Lillian Duncan

This is a work of fiction. Names, characters, places, and incidents either are the product of the author's imagination or are used fictitiously, and any resemblance to actual persons living or dead, business establishments, events, or locales, is entirely coincidental.

PURSUED

COPYRIGHT 2011 by Lillian Duncan

All rights reserved. No part of this book may be used or reproduced in any manner whatsoever without written permission of the author or Pelican Ventures, LLC except in the case of brief quotations embodied in critical articles or reviews.

eBook editions are licensed for your personal enjoyment only. eBooks may not be re-sold, copied or given away to other people. If you would like to share an eBook edition, please purchase an additional copy for each person you share it with.

Contact Information: titleadmin@pelicanbookgroup.com

All scripture quotations, unless otherwise indicated, are taken from the Holy Bible, New International Version(R), NIV(R), Copyright 1973, 1978, 1984 by Biblica, Inc.™ Used by permission of Zondervan. All rights reserved worldwide. www.zondervan.com

Cover Art by *Nicola Martinez*

White Rose Publishing, a division of Pelican Ventures, LLC
www.whiterosepublishing.com PO Box 1738 *Aztec, NM * 87410

White Rose Publishing Circle and Rosebud logo is a trademark of Pelican Ventures, LLC

Publishing History
First White Rose Edition, 2011
Print Edition ISBN 978-1-61116-092-5
Electronic Edition ISBN 978-1-61116-093-2
Published in the United States of America

Dedication

This and all I do is for God's Glory
To friends, then and now.
To Ronny, you are my inspiration always.

This book wouldn't exist if it weren't for my wonderful husband, Ronny, who cooked dinners and ignored the dust bunnies hopping around. My family and friends have been there encouraging more times than they know. Thanks to my mother, Marian Young, Herb, Carol, Blanche, Jay, Barb, Eric, Donna, Didi, Carl, Cork, Bob and all the rest—too many to list by name.
A special thanks to Terry Whalin who took the time to phone a struggling writer and suggest I join American Christian Fiction Writers.
I couldn't have done it without my critique partners so thanks to Candee Fick, Donald Roome, Dianna T. Benson, Virginia Tenery, Lynda Quinn, Fay Lamb, and all the Scribes for their advice, and encouragement.
And to critique partner and friend, Pam Cowart, your help and input on Pursued was invaluable.

No words can express my gratitude to the Creator for all His blessings, big and small.

1

"Unacceptable," Jeffrey Howard whispered.

Heads whipped around as if a bomb had exploded, instead of a whisper.

No, no, no! This can't be happening. Reggie Meyers's insides turned to mush, but she turned towards the head of the table with a smile pasted on her face. She laid the pen down on the contract. It wouldn't do for others to notice her hand shaking. A trembling pen would be a dead giveaway.

"I'm sorry. Did you say unacceptable?" Reggie looked at the owner of Lightning Bolt Enterprises.

"That's what I said." The older man's snow white mustache twitched.

Maybe, it was a joke and he was trying not to smile. She waited for the punch line. It didn't come. If she blew this deal with Lightning Bolt, she'd get fired for sure. Her future at Benton and Greene, Attorneys at Law looked bleak.

"I'm sorry. I don't understand."

The man stood. "I thought you were a lawyer."

"I am—"

He marched over to her. Leaning down, he jabbed at a word. "Right there, can't you see? It says *if* but it should say *when*. It makes the contract unacceptable."

"It's just a clerical error, Mr. Howard. We can cross it out and write in the correct word and initial it. It's no big deal."

"Missy, it may not be a big deal to you, but it is to me. I won't deal with a company that doesn't know the difference between if and when."

Reggie glanced around the table. Not one person looked at her. Not a good sign.

Ignoring his disrespectful tone and words, she spoke again, hoping not to sound like she was begging. She stood, almost nose to nose, except he was over six foot tall and she was a foot shorter. "I'll have a new contract printed up and it will be ready in thirty minutes."

Mr. Howard looked at his watch.

He was going to agree. It would be OK.

He gave the famous lightning bolt smile that had made him and his company renowned. "Sorry, these negotiations are now over." His blue eyes twinkled, then he turned and walked out the room.

Her mouth fell open. Three months of negotiating, over. Just like that. She'd be out looking for another job within the week. Her probationary year wasn't finished yet, so Benton and Greene could do whatever they wanted. *I won't cry in front of all these people.* "I don't understand."

Marta Hagan looked up from the papers she was gathering. "He was a high school English teacher."

****

Cleveland-Hopkins Airport teemed with tired, frustrated, and cranky people as Reggie waited for her luggage at the carousel. *We've forgotten the spirit of thanksgiving.* A tall, blonde curvaceous woman swung an expensive bag over her shoulder, greeting Reggie with a smack.

"Ow!" Reggie touched her forehead expecting the fancy initials to be embedded in her skin. The woman stared down at Reggie's five foot frame. "Oh my! I thought I hit something. Are you OK, sweetie?"

"I'm fine, really." Humiliation stained her face.

Long, tapered fingers tapped Reggie's forehead. "Eww...my bag must have hit you hard. Your forehead matches my nail polish, and I think it's fixing to swell up." Whistling, the woman shook her head. "Darlin', you need some stilettos...you know, elevator shoes?"

"Perhaps. Thanks. I guess these instruments of torture aren't enough." She lifted a foot to show off her cute new heels. Reggie bit her lip. She looked up at the blue sky from the atrium windows encircling the baggage claim area.

A beautiful sight.

The woman looked down. "I sure am sorry about the bump on your noggin."

"It's just a dull ache, I'm sure it'll be fine by morning."

Slinging her long blonde locks behind her, the woman lowered her head and squinted. "I can hardly see it at all. Just a tiny lavender-tint in the center of your forehead. Don't worry, sweetie, you should be home long before it turns dark purple. Come on, follow me." She twirled around and headed towards the luggage bins.

Reggie followed in the blonde's wake. When her suitcase came around, Reggie tugged it off the moving carousel and turned towards her new friend. "Thanks for helping me get through the crowd. Hey, I don't even know your name?"

The woman flicked a wave and glanced back. "Barb."

A grin spread across Reggie's face as she thought about the famous doll and the woman who looked just like that toy. Pulling up the handle of the luggage, she zigzagged her way through the human wall and out to her car.

Her head hurt, but the pain in her feet triumphed. What had possessed her to choose heels on a day spent trudging through crowded airports? Her favorite running shoes would have been a better choice. She rubbed the dull thump in her temple as though it might help her feet and headed out to the parking lot.

Exhausted and hungry, Reggie drummed bright red fingernails on the steering wheel and scowled at the clogged arteries of Cleveland's nightly commuter nightmare. The traffic jam resembled her life, a jumbled out-of-control mess going nowhere. Her mind flashed to the call she'd made to her boss informing them of the failed meeting.

A high school English teacher. As if that explained everything. And as usual, no one at fault, but herself. It wouldn't be fair to blame the assistant who typed up the final contract. It was her responsibility to double check.

It wasn't her first mistake at Benton and Greene, but it might very well be her last.

Reggie sighed. She'd been positive her life would be perfect after accepting her first position as an attorney less than a year before. Sure, she had more money but...but so what?

The car behind her inched up. She glanced at him in her rearview mirror. Coming home from her business trip the Wednesday before Thanksgiving had been a bad idea. The fact that it was a holiday hadn't even crossed her mind.

Checking her watch, she calculated the last time she'd eaten. Reggie leaned over and grabbed her purse. She plunged a hand deep inside, gliding over each item like a woman reading Braille. Frustrated she wiggled her finger into one of the corners. A crisp crackle followed by a stab of stiff plastic gave her hope.

Pulling her hand out, a single wrapped butterscotch dangled from underneath her nail. "Yes!" She fist-pumped the air. A piece of candy would tide her over. She unwrapped the butterscotch, popped it in her mouth, and savored the sweet buttery taste before focusing once again on the traffic.

Spying a hole in the traffic, Reggie pressed against the gas pedal and her car shot off the entrance ramp into the slow lane. She checked her side mirror. She swerved into the middle lane and smiled in victory. One more lane to go.

Thump.

Reggie frowned. A second and a third thump followed. The car shimmied and swayed. Not good. A flat tire? Could this day get any worse? She flipped the right turn signal but nothing happened. Looking over her shoulder, an old beat-up truck lumbered along in the slow lane, but she could make it. She motioned, hoping he would see her. Reggie took a deep breath, and made her move. Tires screeched.

She breathed a sigh of relief. She hadn't heard the thumping noise in the last minute either. Maybe, it wasn't a flat, after—a tiny black and white dog darted out from the bushes at the side of the road and charged into the traffic. She slammed on the brakes.

Reggie looked in the rearview mirror, but all she saw was blue. Panic bubbled up, but before she could react, the truck slammed into her.

Reggie lifted up out of her seat. Each second felt like ten. She moved forward as if swimming in sludge. Her head moved towards the windshield while her body twisted in another direction. *Where was the airb—*

Her head slammed against the window as the car spun out of control. She stomped the brakes, but the car kept spinning. After what seemed like hours, the car jolted to a stop.

Stunned, Reggie sat in her car immobile. Her breath came in little gasps. She lifted her head off the steering wheel and pain ricocheted across her skull. Closing her eyes, Reggie put her head down, working hard to stay calm. *It's a nightmare. The whole lousy day isn't real. This many bad things don't happen to one person in one day. It has to be a dream.*

After a moment, she opened her eyes. Nope, Still in the nightmare.

She inventoried injuries. No blood, thank goodness. After wiggling her toes, she stretched her back. She massaged the spot where her stomach hit the steering wheel. Tender, but not too bad. No serious damage. Everything seemed to be working, but she'd managed to hit her head in the exact same spot as before.

Someone knocked on the window, startling her. Twisting her head, a small moan escaped. Pain shot across her shoulders.

A pair of vibrant blue eyes peered in at her. His mouth moved, but Reggie didn't understand the words. Her head throbbed. He opened her door and bent down closer. "I wanted to know if you're OK."

With measured movements, she lifted her head. Blue eyes, the color of the sun-kissed Caribbean ocean, stared back with concern from underneath a ball cap. Sunlight fanned around his head giving an angelic aura. He smiled, and for a moment, she forgot where she was. Then, she remembered. "You hit me."

His eyes widened in surprise. "You swerved into my lane and didn't use your turn signal. Then, you slammed on the brakes."

Reggie stepped out. The sky dimmed. The whine of cars and eighteen wheelers grew distant and she swayed.

Callused hands clamped onto each arm, guiding her forward until she landed face first, into a chest of red flannel. The shirt smelled of fresh cotton mixed with the muskiness of his cologne. Smelling salts to her senses. Warm, strong arms surrounded her, as she struggled to remain standing.

"Are you all right?"

Horns blared. The squeal of brakes nearby sent a shock of fear through her.

"Do you need a paramedic?" He gave her a gentle shake.

She took a deep, slow breath and exhaled. Another horn sounded, startling her as a car whizzed by. The man's dark hair, curling from under the brim of his hat, flapped in the car's wake, and he shifted his body closer to her car.

He turned his attention to the traffic. "Look, if you're OK, we need to get off the highway before we both get hit. Can you walk?"

"The dog. Where's the dog?"

"I didn't see any dog. You probably imag—"

A boy crawled out of the bushes. "Bootsie!"

Reggie moved out of the man's arms and rushed over to the boy. "You need to stay back. It's not safe out here."

"My dog. His leash broke. I've been chasing him." He wiped tears from his dirt covered face.

"OK, stay calm. I saw him a minute ago."

"There he is. On the other side." The man from the truck announced.

The dog barked as he zeroed in on his boy.

"Oh, no." Reggie moaned. Visions of the dog running into traffic and being smashed in front of this little boy danced in her head.

The truck driver waited for an opening, and then dashed across the highway. Horns rang out, but the cars slowed. He picked up the little black-and-white dog and crossed to where she stood with the little boy. The puppy yapped and clamored to get to his owner.

"OK, now you need to go. This isn't a safe place. Can you find your way home?" Reggie asked.

"I just live right over there." He pointed beyond the bushes. He clasped his dog and ran back with his canine buddy tucked safely under his arm.

"I told you I saw a dog."

"Maybe you should sit down. You don't look so good."

"I think I'm OK." Reggie tugged at her skirt, wishing she'd worn something more comfortable. She hobbled to the back of her car.

"Oh, no." Her beautiful car. Smashed into a bright red accordion. Frowning at the truck driver, she rubbed the trunk. "Look at it."

He shoved the bill of his hat upwards away from his face. "I see it. Looks bad, but at least you weren't seriously hurt."

Taking a step back, she pulled up to her full height. Hands on hips, Reggie turned to the truck driver. "I thought I had a flat tire. I had to get off the road. I waved at you. You should have let me in."

"Do you think people driving down the highway at seventy miles an hour can see into car windows?" He folded his arms and stared down. "Next time, try your turn signal."

"I did, but it must be broken." Biting her lip, she refused to cry. Attorneys were supposed to be tough, not fall apart over every little thing.

"You're lucky you didn't get hurt, but you've got a nasty bump on your head."

"Actually, this happened earlier." She touched the knot.

"Having one of those days, huh?" A slow grin formed as he cleared his throat "Doesn't your car have an airbag?"

"It's supposed to. It—"

"Let me guess…it doesn't work." He looked ready to laugh.

"I guess I didn't do a very good job picking out my first car." She couldn't help but crack a smile, a small one. Dizziness swept over her once again and she reached towards the car for support

"Are you OK? I think you hit your head on the steering wheel. You didn't have your seatbelt on." The man stared at her with concern.

"What are you? The seatbelt police?" Tears welled up. *Just calm down*. It wasn't his fault. She took a deep breath. "I did have my seatbelt on, but it must have came unlatched."

The man shook his head. "I'm sorry, I didn't see the dog, I didn't have time to brake. I wouldn't have hit you if I'd seen him, too.

A police cruiser pulled in behind her ruined car.

2

"I can't believe you're giving me the ticket."

Traffic had resumed its normal pace. They stood off the shoulder of the highway in the grass near the spot where her car had come to rest.

"Sorry, Ma'am."

She waved the citation at him and with her free hand pointed at the driver of the truck. "He hit me from behind. It's his fault, and besides, I couldn't hit the puppy."

"You should never risk your own life for an animal." The truck driver said.

"You're the one who ran across the traffic to get the dog."

"Totally different. I didn't want the little boy to see his dog get hit."

"See, he admits there was a dog." She turned back to the policeman.

The officer's lips curled in a half-hearted smile, his voice polite, but firm. "We've already been through this, ma'am. Hire a lawyer if you want to fight it."

"I am a lawyer."

The two men shared a look.

The officer nodded. "Explains a lot."

The truck driver grinned, but said nothing.

She took a deep breath. *Stay calm. It's the low*

blood sugar making you irritable.

"You may have a problem getting a tow truck the night before Thanksgiving." The officer said.

"I have a headache and I've been traveling all day." Reggie wilted. *Now, what?*

"Look, let's call a truce and let me drive you home, deal?"

She looked at the traffic speeding by, and then at the man's battered old blue truck. The bumpers had more rust than chrome and the windshield had a crack almost as long as the window. She wrinkled her nose.

"Not much to look at, but it gets me where I need to go."

Reggie's face warmed. She hadn't meant to be rude. The man was trying to be helpful. "Right now it looks a lot better than my Beemer, but I'm not in the habit of letting strangers pick me up."

His Caribbean blue eyes twinkled against his tanned skin. "I'm hurt. Really, I am. How can you say we're strangers after all we've been through?"

Looking into his warm eyes, she didn't feel quite as chilled as she had a moment before. Her blood sugar was too low, and her body ached.

The man probably wasn't a serial killer. He was quite handsome in a country sort of way. He was tall and tanned, in spite of the cold weather, and Reggie noticed his broad shoulders in the red flannel shirt he wore. He must be tough—no jacket. His dark brown hair curled over his collar. His faded jeans and cowboy boots looked worn from work, not a fashion statement. He'd be perfect in a tough-guy commercial if he wore a cowboy hat.

"I'm Dylan Monroe and this officer has my name and address." He held out his hand. "If anything happens to you, I'll be the first guy he comes looking for. So, whaddya say?" He pointed at his old truck. "I know it's not a fancy car, but it will get you home."

Reggie turned to the officer. "What do you think?"

"Up to you, ma'am, but I think he's trustworthy. He's never even had a traffic ticket unlike—"

"None of those tickets were my fault."

"It never is." The officer laughed as he walked away. "I'd take you home, but it's out of my jurisdiction. You'll need to have this towed within forty-eight hours or you'll get another ticket. Drive safe and Happy Thanksgiving!"

Another ticket. Reggie turned to the man who was now her rescuer. "Are you sure you don't mind driving me home? I don't want to be a bother." It had been a long time since lunch. She assessed her physical condition, clammy hands and dizziness.

"You a bother? No way." The man had a sense of humor.

"I'll need my luggage." She looked at her car. The trunk lid was half-open and smashed in.

"Let's see if we can open your trunk. Then, I can get you home. If you don't mind me saying, you look more tired than a groundhog in February."

He talked like a cowboy, too.

"I am exhausted. It's been a long, long day." She reached in her purse and pulled out a twenty.

"For your trouble."

"I don't do favors for money. A simple thank you will be enough."

It was getting warmer by the minute in spite of the chill of the day. "Well...well, thanks for your help." She stuffed the money back in her purse, feeling as if she'd insulted the man.

"You're welcome. Always glad to help a damsel in distress." He tipped his hat and bowed. His clear blue eyes crinkled as he smiled.

"I'm Reggie Meyers." She held out her own hand. He engulfed her hand in both of his. He held it, not letting go after the shake. His warmth made her shiver.

"It's nice to meet you, Reggie. Short for Regina?"

She nodded.

"Regina is such a beautiful name. It fits you perfectly."

She opened her mouth but had no idea what to say. Instead, she pulled her hand back from his.

After using a crowbar, Dylan yanked her luggage from the crumpled trunk and headed for the truck. His walk was confident. He seemed sure of his place in this world

Reggie watched him place her luggage in the truck bed. She envied him. It was exhausting always second-guessing herself, never being sure about the right way to act, never sure what people thought of her, always worried about the impression she made. She walked to the passenger side of the truck. She reached, but Dylan's hand came around and opened the door before she could.

"You might need a hand there." Dylan said, in a slow drawl.

Looking at the height of the truck and then down at her own tight skirt and heels. It could be a problem but she was quite capable of getting into a truck without this cowboy's help. "I can do it."

"Suit yourself." He walked to the driver's side.

Lifting a leg to get in, her foot stopped a few inches short of where it needed to be. Reggie tried hopping in with no success. She peeked at Dylan, sitting in the driver's seat, pretending not to notice her struggles. After a quick glance around, she hiked her skirt and pulled up into the truck.

CDs without cases and empty gum wrappers littered the seat and floor. Dylan picked up a pack of sugar-free mint gum and held it out to her. When she shook her head, he pulled out two slices, unwrapped them, and popped both in his mouth.

"Trying to quit smoking. It's been tough, but I think I've got it licked."

"How long since you stopped?"

"Three months." He pointed at the gum packs. "I've got a three pack a day habit. I'm thinking of buying stock in the chewing gum company."

"Not a bad idea. I might look into it myself."

"Buckle up." Dylan chuckled.

"You really are the seatbelt police, aren't you? I hope this works better than mine did." She muttered, as she fastened it.

As Dylan drove, Reggie called to arrange for a tow truck to pick up her car and take it to a repair shop. Within fifteen minutes, Dylan pulled up to her apartment.

The complex consisted of duplexes nestled into the woods adjoining the Cleveland Metroparks system. Built to blend in with the environment, they were shingled with rustic brown wood siding.

"This is where you live?" He shook his head. "Can't imagine living with all these people around. It would drive me nuts."

"I love it. It's great. It has a pool, a sauna, hot tub and tennis courts." She hadn't used any of the amenities since she'd moved in. The goal of becoming a junior partner took all her time.

"To each his own. I'm just a simple country boy."

"Well, thanks for the ride." She opened the door and slid out of the truck, but winced as her feet landed on the concrete. She may never wear heels again. She wondered what her boss would think about her going to court in jogging shoes, but then realized it could be a moot point. They would probably fire her anyway after losing the Lightning Bolt contract.

By the time Reggie rearranged her skirt, Dylan was beside her holding her luggage. She reached to take it from him, but he held on tight.

"I'll carry it."

"I can handle it." She grabbed at the handle but only managed to latch on to his hand. Warmth emanated from Dylan. She yanked her hand back.

"I'm sure you can, but my mama raised a gentleman."

Staring into those blue eyes, Reggie saw

resistance would be futile. She told him the number and pointed towards her home. She had no energy left. She followed, glad he couldn't see her limping.

Dylan turned and waved towards her door. "Were you expecting someone?"

The door stood ajar.

3

Reggie stared at the door, then at Dylan, her breath coming faster. She shook her head.

He put a finger to his lips and pushed her aside.

Her eyes strained to see through the darkened room. Was someone still inside? She trembled. Fear, combined with low blood sugar, was a recipe for disaster.

"Stay here while I check the situation out. " His warm, minty breath tickled her ear as he whispered, reminding her she wasn't alone.

She nodded and backed away from the door, thankful Dylan was there.

He eased her luggage to the ground and moved to the opposite side of the door. Drawing back one booted foot, he pushed the door wider. Dylan slipped into her apartment with the stealth of a tiger.

Reggie shivered, unsure if it was from the cold, or from fear. In spite of the chill, her palms turned clammy. Putting hands in her coat pockets, she turned away from the wind. Her mind flashed back to the day she'd left for her trip.

After putting luggage in the car, she'd walked back to the door and jiggled the knob to double check. It had definitely been locked. She stomped feet trying to keep them from freezing.

Where was Dylan? Was the intruder still in her apartment? Maybe he'd been knocked unconscious or was being held at gunpoint? She should go check. Three more minutes. Much to her relief, two minutes later, Dylan appeared in the doorway, his face grim.

"It's OK. No one's here but—"

Before Dylan could finish, Reggie barged past him and into her apartment. Her mouth dropped open and her steps froze.

Chunks and slivers of treasured figurines lay strewn on the floor. Her beautiful white leather sofa looked like a dead Polar bear. Guts of stuffing protruded from the slashed fabric. Cushions floated like white icebergs among the living room debris.

Her beautiful apartment trashed. A spark of anger ignited in the pit of her stomach. Trent must have lost his mind. What had he been thinking to break into her apartment and do this?

"Better call the cops." Dylan's voice broke into her racing thoughts. He walked over to the door and peered at the lock.

Dylan was right, of course. Calling the cops made sense, but what would be the point? Accusing Trent would do nothing but aggravate the situation. The scenario played out in her mind. After dating for several months, Trent's fingerprints littered her apartment. He'd simply deny any wrongdoing and being the upright citizen, they would believe him. "There isn't anything they can do. I don't even know when this happened. I've been gone for two we—"

"Someone trashed your place. And apparently, they had a key, or you forgot to lock the door because it doesn't show signs of a break-in. You can't just ignore this."

"Yes, I can. You got me home and I appreciate it, but I would like you to go now." Reggie blinked back tears. Her voice trembled, but she refused to cry in front of this handsome stranger. She'd handled much worse than a little apartment bashing. No need to fall apart.

"I am not leaving you like this." Beneath the quiet voice was a hint of steel.

She glared at him, resenting the sympathy in his voice. She didn't need his pity or his protection. "I can take care of myself. Just go or I'll call the police and tell them you're harassing me."

"Great idea. And while you're at it, you might want to tell them someone broke into your apartment." He smiled sweetly at her.

She cracked a grim smile and took a deep breath. "Very funny." She moved from the living room to the doorway of the kitchen. She wrinkled her nose at the unpleasant odor. Flour and sugar covered the counters and floor. Broken eggs had oozed off the counter and dried into hard globs on the tile. Flies swarmed around the foul smelling concoction.

She eyed the broken shards of dishes scattered about. Her expensive china, chopped into hundreds of tiny pieces, gave a mosaic look to the kitchen table and counters. Was there anything left in her cupboards? The time she'd spent choosing the perfect pattern flashed in her mind. Down the drain.

Her breath quickened. She straightened and turned back to the cowboy who shadowed her every step. He watched her with compassion and concern. She took a deep breath.

Even though she'd caused the accident he'd been nothing but kind to her. No reason to yell at Dylan. He'd been a perfect gentleman. The accident seemed so important just a few moments before, but not any longer.

"I'm sorry, I shouldn't be yelling at you. It's just..." Her words faltered.

"Can't say I blame you. It's been a rough few hours." He smiled as he pulled out another stick of gum. He stuck the empty wrapper in his pocket.

She managed a smile. "Still, I don't need to take it out on—"

Reggie swayed, feeling the familiar weakness coming. Her head began to spin. She took a step towards the sofa, but lost her balance and crumpled to the floor in the middle of a pile of fiberfill.

"Are you OK?" Dylan knelt beside her.

"Need sugar." She mumbled.

He found a bottle of apple juice in the fridge and popped the top, then lifted it to her lips. After several sips, she grasped it with shaking hands.

Her mind cleared as the sugar worked its magic. Horrified and embarrassed to let this stranger see her weak and vulnerable, she pushed Dylan's hand from her shoulder. "I'm OK, now. I'm fine."

"Diabetic?"

Nodding, Reggie stared around the room. From her spot on the living room floor, it looked even worse. She gave in to the tears. This was too much. A lost contract, a car accident, and now this.

Trent had known just what to do to hurt her. She loved this place. Her first real home. And now he'd ruined it for her. Her tears subsided.

"Ready to call the police?" Dylan's voice was quiet.

"You don't understand. It would only make things worse. I just...I just..." She shook her head. She closed her eyes and put both hands to her head. Squeezing back tears, she massaged her temples. *It will be OK. You've survived worse things than this, and You'll survive this.*

Dylan interrupted her internal pep talk. "I've got an idea. You obviously need to eat something, and you aren't going to be doing any cooking here anytime soon. Let's go find some grub. I could eat a horse."

She wanted to tell him to just go away, that she could take care of herself. But the truth was she didn't think she could. Her logical mind told her to make him leave, but she didn't want to be alone.

Things would be better after she ate. A little sustenance would give her the stamina to face this disaster. She nodded. "Let me change clothes and check my sugar level and I'll be right back."

Dylan held out both hands. She placed her hands in his and he pulled her up. Remembering earlier when his arms had held her after the accident, she fought the urge to lean against him. It would feel so nice to have his arms around her.

She stepped back and let go of him. "Does the bedroom look..." She took a deep breath. "look this bad?"

He nodded. "Worse."

Reggie steeled herself as she walked to the bedroom.

****

Dylan watched Reggie walk into her bedroom, her back ramrod straight. She was one tough lady. Tough, beautiful, and sexy. Feisty, but he liked feisty.

He couldn't just leave Reggie here to deal with this mess alone. She hadn't called anyone at the accident scene to come pick her up. So, maybe she didn't have a boyfriend, if he was blessed.

His gaze roved around the trashed room.

Probably an angry ex-boyfriend by the looks of her apartment. The person had a key.

Just like Daniella. The familiar pain slashed through his heart, as it always did when he thought of his little sister. He should have known she needed him. He hadn't helped Daniella, but he could help Reggie.

He inspected the room more carefully. The walls were pristine white and the woodwork was a dark cherry or mahogany. A breakfast bar separated the living room from the kitchen and dining area. It was feminine, but not too girly-girly.

The only knickknacks were those little statue things. They must've been on the set of shelves in a corner of the living room. A white leather sofa and two matching chairs were the center point of the room. He didn't see a TV, but he did see a beautiful mahogany cabinet he guessed held one.

He sat on the arm of the chair to wait. He fished around in his pocket for a stick of gum, but found none. Why would Reggie refuse to call the cops? A lawyer should know what to do, but it wasn't his place to interfere.

He wouldn't mind getting to know her better. Something about her touched him. She'd been a pistol after the accident, but cried like a baby over broken figurines and spilled milk. There was more to Reggie than the tough exterior she showed the world.

He had to find out what happened and who was responsible. Reggie needed his help whether she would admit it or not. And Dylan never backed away from a challenge.

Maybe God orchestrated this whole thing. Could this be one of those divine appointments his preacher always talked about?

He smiled. A divine appointment with Reggie. Maybe, a divine date could be arranged if he played his cards right. Of course, right now, what she really needed was a friend and that he could do, if she let him.

Reggie walked back in the room. She'd changed into a pair of designer jeans and a silky green blouse. Her shiny black hair draped loosely on her shoulders. Her ridiculous heels were replaced with comfortable-looking loafers.

Dylan whistled. "You look great."

Reggie gave a weak smile. "Liar."

4

Slumped in a booth at her favorite deli, Reggie stared at Dylan, not quite sure why she was having dinner with this handsome stranger. She was grateful for his kindness.

Discovering Trent had trashed her apartment had been more than she could handle. Tapping her red manicured nails on the cheap yellow Formica table top, she glanced over at Dylan. He continued to stare at the menu even though they'd already ordered.

Her menu lay unopened, she knew it by heart. She stopped by two or three times every week. The food was healthy and tasty. Just the smell of the chicken noodle soup revived her spirits. She cleared her throat.

He looked up from the menu, his jaw working on the latest piece of gum.

"It's very kind of you to bring me here. Especially after the way I've been acting. I'm sure you have better things to do than babysitting the crazy woman who crashed into you."

"Are you kidding?" His deep blue eyes twinkled. "This'll make a great story tomorrow at Thanksgiving dinner. Besides, I gotta eat and the scenery is amazing."

"You need glasses. I feel like a train ran over

me." She ripped open a pack of crackers and nibbled.

"Wait 'til tomorrow. You'll feel like that train ran over you then put it in reverse." His voice turned serious. "I know it's none of my business, but what's going on? Why don't you want to call the police?"

Reggie couldn't avoid the question. Dylan deserved an explanation. He'd risked his life going into the dark apartment. "It's nothing dramatic. I broke up with my boyfriend right before I left on a business trip. I guess he was more upset than I realized."

"I'd say he was more than a little upset. "And you don't call the cops because…?"

"They wouldn't find any real proof. It would end up being a case of he said, she said. Besides, he just made a mistake." Avoiding Dylan's eyes, she reached over and pulled out a napkin from the dispenser.

"Crimes aren't mistakes. He's the one who did the crime. Let him pay for it."

Dylan was right, of course. She would advise a client exactly the same, but it wasn't cut and dried when you were the one involved and it could ruin Trent's career. She didn't want that laid at her doorstep. It would just make matters worse.

"I know you're right but…" She shredded the paper napkin as she spoke.

"Looks like you did the right thing by kicking him to the curb. Are you afraid of him?"

"No. Well, maybe." Her pulse picked up. "The police could pick him up, but there's no real proof he did it. And then, he'd be really mad. I don't know what he'd do."

"Reggie, I won't let him touch you. You're safe with me." Dylan's voice turned angry.

Wow! He seemed genuinely concerned for her. How she longed to have someone in her life to lean on. Someone who would love her. But a boot-scootin' cowboy wasn't what she had in mind. Her mister would be the tall, dark, sophisticated type, complete with briefcase.

"I'm sure he regrets doing it." She tossed the shredded napkin on the table and reached for another.

"Not enough to clean up the mess he made before you got home." Dylan pointed out. "Or to call and warn you about his little mistake."

"He really is a nic—"

"Nice guys don't do those kinds of things." Dylan's voice turned angry.

Startled by his tone, Reggie wondered where the anger came from. Had he experienced stalking? Besides, it wasn't really stalking, it was Trent venting anger, a one-time event. She'd make sure of that.

"I'm not trying to defend his actions but why ruin his life over it? Everyone loses their temper now and then. I'll make sure he leaves me alone after this."

Before Dylan could answer, the waitress interrupted the conversation and placed the bowl of chicken soup in front of Reggie. It landed with a thud, sloshing on the table. Reggie looked up to complain but the woman's attention was focused elsewhere—on Dylan.

The waitress leaned low—much lower than

necessary—to place Dylan's plate in front of him. "Anything else I can do for you, let me know." Her voice was low and throaty.

The waitress stepped away from their table.

"I can't believe it." Reggie sputtered.

"Believe what?"

"The way she flirted with you."

He winked and reached for his sandwich. "Made you jealous, did it?"

"Of course not." She ignored the warm flush of embarrassment on her face. "I've only known you for an hour, but she doesn't know that. That's all I'm saying."

"Sure it is. Sure it is." He winked at her.

She daintily dipped her spoon into the soup while Dylan tore into his corned beef sandwich. His hair fell across his forehead. When he came up for air, he muttered something about delicious between mouthfuls. After Dylan finished his sandwich, coleslaw and pickle, he motioned for the waitress and ordered two slices of cheesecake.

"I can't eat cheesecake—my sugar level would go too high." Reggie reminded him.

"I know. They're both for me."

Reggie laughed.

The man sure liked to eat.

****

"I meant what I said, Reggie. He's not going to lay a hand on you. "Now, we need to come up with a plan." He took a bite of cheesecake.

"A plan for what?" Reggie put down her spoon

He held up a fork full of the cheesecake. "Tastes great. A plan for you, of course. You can't stay at your apartment tonight and tomorrow's a holiday so...you need a plan."

"I can stay in a hotel tonight, and tomorrow my plan will be cleaning up my apartment."

The boyfriend could come back. She might think the guy was over being angry but there was no way to know. He might have more revenge on his mind. If something happened to her, Dylan wouldn't be able to forgive himself.

"But it's Thanksgiving. Didn't you have plans for the holiday?"

"Not everyone has Norman Rockwell holidays." Reggie's eyes filled with tears, but they didn't fall. "Truthfully, I didn't even think about Thanksgiving. I was going to stay home and get caught up on my laundry."

"Doesn't sound like much fun."

"I'll be fine at the hotel. I can make arrangements for a rental car and..."

"No good." He frowned at her then held up his hand. "I have an idea." He pulled his cell phone out of his pocket.

"What are you doing, Dylan?"

He held up his hand again. "Hey, Sis. It doesn't look like I'm going to make it to church tonight."

"Why not?" His sister's voice was curious.

"It's a long story. I'll tell you about it later but I need a favor. I've got a friend here and I thought she could spend the night with..."

Reggie began shaking her head. "No, no. I can't do...I don't..."

Dylan ignored her. "Thanks, we'll be there when we get there." He hung up the phone and smiled. "It's all arranged. You can stay at my sister's tonight and have Thanksgiving Dinner with us tomorrow. Bright and early Friday, I'll drive you back and we can clean up the mess."

"No. No. I'm not going— It's just ridiculous."

"Why is it ridiculous?"

"You just don't invite strangers to your sister's house for Thanksgiving dinner. I don't know you or your family. I can't impose on you."

"Not a problem. You're not imposing, I invited you. Come on." He'd convince her to call the police later but it could wait until later. "It'll be fun. You'll have a great time. Do you like kids?"

"I suppose so."

"Good. My sister's got five of them. You'll have a great time."

"Five kids. Wow. I don't know anyone who has more than two kids."

"Great, then. It's all settled."

"I don't even know where you live." She said in exasperation.

"Did you ever hear of Fredericksburg?"

"Sure, it's in Virginia. I am not going to Virginia tonight, Dylan. I don't care what you say."

"Fredericksburg, Ohio. It's a small town in Wayne County. About an hour south of here."

"What were you doing in Cleveland if you live so far away?"

"Took some friends to the airport. They're flying to Cancun for the weekend. I thought about going with them, but just couldn't give up my

Thanksgiving turkey and pumpkin pie." He scooped up the last bite of the cheesecake.

"You know it's very nice of you to invite me, but I just can't go off somewhere with a stranger."

"Reggie, Reggie, don't you know a stranger's just a friend you haven't met yet?"

"What century are you living in, Dylan? People don't do things like this anymore."

He winked. "They do where I come from."

5

A concussion, Reggie decided. It had to be the explanation for why at this very moment she sat beside this handsome stranger in his beat-up truck going to his sister's house for Thanksgiving. How had he talked her into this? She didn't do bizarre spur-of-the-moment things like this.

Definitely, a concussion. Maybe she should ask Dylan to take her to the hospital for an MRI before going to his sister's. She sneaked a peak at him.

With both hands on the steering wheel, his eyes moved from the rearview mirror to the side mirror, then to the road in front.

She peered down at the speedometer. Exactly fifty-five miles per hour. His following the driving rules so precisely made her want to scream. Her brain urged her to tell him to go sixty or fifty-nine, anything but fifty-five. So far, she'd managed to keep her mouth shut, but driving slow made her nuts.

They hadn't talked much on the drive. Her mind kept flashing back to her trashed apartment. She couldn't believe Trent had done such a thing. Sure, she'd broken up with him, but she'd been very nice about it, giving him the *it's not you, it's me* speech. Apparently, he hadn't bought it. She forced her thoughts from Trent and turned to Dylan.

"Is something wrong? You seem agitated."

"Just making sure we aren't being followed. We don't know for sure who ransacked your apartment, and the last thing I want is to put my sister and her family in danger."

"You're right, Dylan. I didn't even think of that." She reached over and touched his hand. Warm and rough. Her body, melted like ice cream on a hot day. In just a few hours, he'd managed to make her feel safe for the first time in her life. "I shouldn't go. Just take me back home, please."

He shook his head. "Not going to happen. No one's going to be able to follow us without my knowing. As soon as we get to my neck of the woods, I'll make sure of it. Nothing's going to happen to you or to my sister."

"Are you sure? I don't mind going home."

"I'm sure." He took his eyes off the road for a moment and looked at her. He wasn't going to change his mind.

"So, what do you do?"

"Me? A little bit of this and that, but mostly I'm a farmer."

"A farmer." *Not a cowboy, but close.* She'd known his calloused hands didn't carry a briefcase. Her first encounter with a real-life agriculturist. What could they possibly have in common? Tomorrow might be a very long day. "What kind of farming?" She asked, using a cheerful and interested tone.

"Dairy farming."

"Cows." Definitely out of her area of

expertise. Glancing at Dylan, Reggie found him staring at her with a knowing smile on his face. Almost as if he could read her mind. "How nice."

"So, Madame Lawyer, what kind of law do you practice?"

"A little of this and a little of that, but mostly I work with business contracts." Reggie didn't want to give Dylan a long drawn out explanation he probably wouldn't care about, anyway.

"How nice."

Catching his humor, she laughed. "I guess we live in different worlds, don't we?"

He flipped on his turn signal and then exited the highway. Pointing at the blinkers, he looked at her with a mischievous grin. "That's how you use a turn signal. Of course, it helps when it's in working order."

"Thanks for the driving lesson." She grinned back.

"My pleasure. I'll be glad to give you a few more if you want. After all safety is a very good thing."

"I suppose so."

Dylan held up a pack of gum, but she shook her head. He pulled out a stick for himself. "Where was your business meeting at?"

"Indianapolis. What a disaster." Grabbing her throat, she pretended to choke. She went on to explain the minute mistake. When she finished, she looked over at him. "Can you believe it? An English teacher."

"He sure seems nicer in his commercials."

"Because he wants your money." She giggled. "But he did smile at me as he told me." She looked over at him a moment. "Can I ask you a question, Dylan?"

"Shoot. My life's an open book."

"Why did you really invite me to your sister's?"

"Mmm. Good question."

Staring out into the darkened countryside, she wondered if he would tell her the truth. It was obvious there was more to his invitation than her holiday plans.

"I was worried about you. Plain and simple. This Trent may not be quite as nice as you think."

"He wouldn't hurt me."

"Yeah, that's what my sister thought, too."

Her heart dropped a beat. "Your sister?"

"Yeah, my baby sister. Her name was Daniella."

Was. Reggie heard the word and knew this story didn't have a happy ending. "I'm sorry, Dylan. You don't have to talk about it."

"I think I do. You're not taking this apartment trashing seriously enough. Daniella was away at college and had a boyfriend there. When she broke up with him, he refused to believe it. The situation went from bad to worse. She finally called my dad and told him what was going on. We went down right away to bring her home." He stopped talking and kept his eyes straight ahead on the road. His Adam's apple bobbed. Silence filled the truck. He looked back at her. "But when we got there, he'd broken into her dorm room. Shot her and then himself."

"Oh, Dylan. How horrible. Did she...did she..."

"Yes, she died. Everyone loved Daniella. Beautiful and funny and smart. She kicked around the idea of becoming a lawyer. And she would have been a good one. When we'd argue, she always won. Mom and Dad to her side." He adjusted his rearview mirror. "I sure do miss her."

"I am so sorry."

"You've got to be careful, Reggie."

She nodded. No wonder Dylan had been so protective.

For several minutes they drove in silence on dark country roads. Soon more and more houses sprinkled the landscape, and twinkling lights in the distance announced the next town.

"Fredericksburg?"

"Hardly, this is the big city of Wooster."

"Woohoo for Wooster." It was weird, but even with everything going on, she felt happy.

"Fredericksburg is a tad smaller. Have you ever heard of Wooster? It's small but we actually make the news from time to time."

"I'm not from this area. I moved to Ohio for my job, and haven't had much time to explore the rest of the state."

"Too bad. Ohio's a great place to live, lots to do. "

"I suppose." She didn't tell him she didn't care where she lived as long as she stayed on the fast track to partnership. A partnership meant security and money. She'd never known the luxury of security, but now she was determined to get it and keep it. It was the reason she'd chosen the law as her career.

As they drove out of Wooster, darkness

returned. It overwhelmed her. Living in the city with all the lights, it never got completely dark. Not like this. She couldn't see her hand in front of her face out here. "What is that?" She wrinkled her nose.

"Manure. Some farmer must have fertilized his field." He chuckled.

Definitely country.

"I haven't seen anything suspicious, but just in case someone's trying to follow, we're going to do a bit of creative driving." He turned right without signaling. As soon as he'd turned, the car surged forward. Chunks of gravel pinged against the underside of the truck. He turned right once again and drove even faster.

She gripped the armrest. "And you thought I was a bad driver."

"I know what I'm doing." He made a left turn. "Not a car in sight."

She looked behind.

He was right.

She turned back in her seat in time to see a shape emerge out of the darkness. "What's that?" She squinted and yelped.

"Amish buggy, a lot of Amish live in the area," he said, as he expertly pulled around the slow moving vehicle.

Turning in her seat, she stared. She'd never seen an Amish buggy up close.

"OK, here comes the big city of Fredericksburg. Don't blink or you might miss it."

"I'm sure you're exaggerating." She laughed.

But he wasn't. Less than a minute later, they were on their way back out of town. They drove up a hill Dylan called South Hill and into a housing development, just like ones in any suburb of Cleveland.

Dylan clicked his turn signal and turned into the drive of a blue-trimmed, brick home with a one-car garage attached to it. Dylan parked and then hopped out of the truck. As Reggie opened her door, Dylan stood waiting. He held up his arms to her. She hesitated for a moment but then slid into them.

He swung her with ease from the truck and placed her gently on the ground. She liked the feel of his arms around her. She wouldn't have minded him lingering for a moment longer.

"There you go."

"Thanks." She muttered, glad of the darkness so Dylan couldn't see the the effects of warmth in her cheeks. "Sir Galahad."

"At your service, my fair lady." He turned to the bed of his truck and lifted out her suitcase.

Before they made it to the house, the door opened and a slightly plump woman bounced out to greet them. Dylan was instantly cocooned in her chubby arms. He gave her a big hug back.

"Hey, Sis. I want you to meet a friend of mine."

She stood a little taller than Reggie. She wore a faded yellow apron covered in flour. It read, 'happier than a pig in mud.' Dylan's sister turned towards Reggie with a smile that transformed her from a tired, overworked housewife into a beauty queen.

Her smile reminded Reggie of Dylan's, just as sweet and as genuine.

She wiped her hands on her apron and reached out to shake Reggie's hand. "Hi, I'm Joni. J-o-n-i. And yes, if you happen to be thinking Bob Dylan and Joni Mitchell. You're on the right track. Our parents are old hippies who are still obsessed with the sixties."

Reggie couldn't help but like Joni.

"I'm so glad Dylan brought you down for the holiday." Joni pulled her up the porch steps and into the house. "Miracle of miracles. The kids are asleep. So, we'll actually be able to talk for a few minutes, but we'll have to do it in the kitchen. I'm doing a little baking for tomorrow."

"I really appreciate—"

"Don't think another thing about it. A friend of my brother is a friend of mine."

The smell of baked apples drifted from the kitchen as they made their way through the living room. The kitchen was almost the size of Reggie's whole apartment. It was painted bright yellow and sunflowers were everywhere. Sunflower border, sunflower plaques, sunflower canisters.

It looked like summer and felt like home.

Joni indicated the chairs at the kitchen table but she went back to the center island. A big hunk of dough sat amidst a circle of flour. Dylan plopped himself onto a stool and motioned for her to do the same.

"What are you making?" Reggie asked as she perched on the other stool.

"Pies. I got a little behind on my baking so I'm determined to finish them tonight before I go to bed. If I don't, I won't be able to relax enough to sleep. All I'll be thinking about is, I should be making pies."

"Really, you're making pies from scratch. I've never seen anybody do that before."

She looked up to find both Joni and Dylan staring at her as if she were from another planet.

"Didn't your mom bake, Reggie?" Joni asked.

Reggie took a deep breath. "I wouldn't have any idea. My mom deserted me when I was four."

A myriad of emotions played out on Joni's face. Horror, then sadness, but then her face settled into compassion. "I'm sorry. I didn't mean to bring up a sad subject. Come on over here and let me show you how you make a pie."

"Don't apologize. It was a long time ago."

"Still, it couldn't have been easy." Joni said.

Faces flashed through Reggie's mind. Faces of foster parents and siblings she'd learned to love, only to leave them all sooner or later. Home after home hadn't worked out. She'd learned to rely on herself. Trusting others only made for more hurt and misery.

"I suppose. But you know the saying, 'what doesn't kill us makes us stronger.' 'That's my motto." Thinking of her apartment, her gaze met Dylan's. She saw respect and encouragement in his. Although, it pleased her, it frightened her, as well.

"Good attitude, Reggie. So, how did you meet my brother?"

"Let me tell you how we met, Sis. You aren't going to believe this." Dylan interrupted. He looked at Reggie with arched eyebrows as if asking for permission.

She nodded. She knew he would enjoy telling

this story.

Dylan proceeded to tell of their inopportune meeting. His brother-in-law came in during the story and perched on a stool. After making introductions, Dylan continued making everyone laugh as he retold it from the beginning.

"Only my brother-in-law could manage to be in a car accident and end up with the second prettiest girl in Ohio. With my wife being the prettiest, of course." Richard laughed.

"Liar." Joni flicked floured fingers towards him.

"Am not. As far as I'm concerned, I'm the luckiest man in the world. God's blessed me with you." He came up behind her and nuzzled her neck.

"Don't mind him, Reggie. He's a hopeless romantic." Joni giggled.

Reggie thought they might be the sweetest couple she'd ever seen.

Richard took his seat and looked over at Dylan. "Did you hear about the Stark farm?"

"No."

"It went into foreclosure last week."

"You're kidding. I knew they were having a rough time after the spring drought, but I didn't know it was that bad." Dylan grabbed an apple from the fruit bowl and bit into it.

"Guess it was." Richard looked at the group. "I hate to break up the party but six AM comes mighty early. I've got to get some sleep if I'm going to take those boys of mine huntin' tomorrow."

"Reggie's staying here tonight so we're going

to sleep in the spare room." Joni said.

"No, no. I can sleep in the spare room. I don't want to put you out."

Joni looked up from filling the pie pan with an apple and walnut mixture. "No way. You get our room so you can have your own bathroom. Believe me when I say you don't want to share the bathroom with the heathens. Oops...I mean our wonderful children."

"That's for sure. Nice to meet you, Reggie." Richard gave a wave and left.

Reggie watched as Joni carefully laid the dough on top of the apples and used her fingers to crimp the edges of the dough. Joni's face was radiant. Love for her family oozed from her pores. The simple act of Joni baking a pie for her family brought an overwhelming sense of loneliness to Reggie. She choked back tears.

This was the family from her dreams. Where they lived happily ever after. Only this wasn't her family, it was Dylan's. She didn't belong here or anywhere.

6

Stretching, Reggie opened her eyes, her gaze finding the clock. *Wow!* Already past nine o'clock. She never slept past five thirty even on weekends. She grimaced as she sat up. Every inch of her body hurt.

The bizarre events of the previous day played out in her mind. She reached up, touching the goose egg on her forehead. It must look hideous.

As she waited for the pain to subside, she realized Joni had a wonderful sense of decorating. A mixture of the old and the new made the room both comforting and fashionable. The bed was an antique roller with a beautiful handmade quilt. The other furniture was antique, but the modern art paintings added zing.

The vibrant colors brightened Reggie's mood. She limped over to a small picture of a little girl with long golden hair, standing at a well. The thick gold frame accented the child's hair. Down in the corner, just below the well in beautiful flowing calligraphy, was the name Joni. She checked another painting and found the same.

Amazing. Who would have thought the pie-baking mother of five had time to be such a talented artist? Reggie had minored in art as an undergrad, but picked a more practical field for her career. The law didn't allow for creativity but it provided other more important things. Stability and security.

She sat on the bed enjoying Joni's talent for another moment, before heading to the bathroom. A shower and some aspirin in the medicine cabinet helped with the soreness. At least, she'd packed casual clothes rather than her usual business suits. The thought of wearing her normal tailored pantsuits made her muscles ache.

She slipped on black jeans and a slinky, teal blue long sleeved shirt with a draped neck and front. She brushed out her hair and considered putting in her normal ponytail, but rejected the idea. The band would just make her headache worse.

After dressing, Reggie ventured out. Voices from the kitchen drifted down the hall. "Have you called Bobbie Jo and told her you have company?"

"Why? She won't care. I keep telling you we're just friends."

At the sound of Dylan's voice, Reggie's footsteps halted. Who was this Bobbie Jo? Not that she cared if Dylan had a girlfriend, but she was curious. She looked around, feeling guilty for eavesdropping, but her curiosity proved to be a greater force than her will.

"Friends? Are you sure? Somehow I don't think Bobbie Jo got the memo."

Dylan's boots scraped the hardwood floor as if he might be pacing.

A timer buzzed and Reggie heard Joni open the oven. Reggie's stomach gripped tight with hunger. Her blood sugar must be low.

"Just friends or not, you better call her up and warn her. You can't just go over there toting another woman without telling her."

"Fine. I'll take my business outside, unless you want to be my secretary and call for me?"

"I don't want to be anywhere around when you tell her about your cute little girlfriend."

"Don't be ridiculous. I just met her. She needs my help right now, and that's all there is."

"You are such a moron."

A door slammed shut. Dylan must have left. After counting to ten, Reggie rounded the corner with a smile pasted on her face. Bowls and pans covered the countertops, yellow peeked through but just barely. Every burner of the stove had a pan on it.

Reggie sniffed with appreciation. The aroma of baked turkey made her mouth water. She could understand why Dylan chose this over Cancun. "My goodness you've been busy. It smells great."

"Thanks. How are you feeling?" Joni headed over to the coffee pot with a mug in her hand.

"Pretty sore. Every part of my body hurts."

"Oh Reggie, your forehead is swollen. Ouch, it looks bad."

"I'll survive."

"I'm sure you will." Joni patted Reggie's hand. "How'd you sleep?"

"Just fine. I can't believe I slept so late. I saw your paintings." Her gaze strayed to the deck. Dylan paced the perimeter with a cell phone to his ear. "They're amazing. You're very talented."

"Those things. Just an experiment gone wrong." Joni laughed as she handed Reggie a cup of steaming coffee. "I've tried to throw them out, but Richard refuses. That's why they're hidden in the bedroom. Cream and sugar?"

"No thanks, I drink it black." She took a sip and smiled. "Mmm. Good."

"We only eat a light breakfast on Thanksgiving." Joni pointed at some rolls and a box of cereal. "Take your pick."

"Cereal, please." She walked over to the box, but her gaze strayed towards the sweet rolls. "Oooh, those rolls look great."

"Yeah, nothing like bakery goodies. Go ahead. It's Thanksgiving. You're allowed to pig out."

"I'm diabetic. It's under control, but if I eat one of those it might not be." Reggie sighed, looked at the boxes of cereal, and picked the generic corn flakes. She couldn't believe how relaxed she felt around Joni. It usually took months before she could open up.

"Maybe I should cook something special for you for dinner?"

"Not necessary. I can eat what everyone else eats. I just have to make the right choices and watch the amounts." She poured flakes into a bowl, but kept her attention on the deck, wondering how his phone call was going. "Do you still paint, Joni?"

"When I have time. Richard even built me a little studio out back and put up a sign that says 'no children allowed.' Not that they listen."

"Did you have formal training?"

"Not really. I planned on majoring in art at college but I majored in kids instead." Joni shrugged as she cracked an egg and added it the mixture of cornbread. "And I wouldn't change my decision for the world."

"I minored in art, but chose to focus on a job to pay the rent instead." Reggie had expected the house to be noisy with five kids, but she didn't hear them anywhere. "The kids still sleeping?"

"The boys went out hunting with Richard." Joni plunged her hands in the cornbread mixture kneading it.

"How old are they?" Kids, hunting with real guns? They must be older than she realized.

Dylan turned and waved at her, then stomped off the porch. He must be having an interesting conversation.

"Nine, eleven and twelve." Joni's voice drew Reggie's attention.

"You let them have guns?"

"Sure, they all passed the gun safety course."

Reggie knew farms had to have guns for…snakes and predators. Farmers must train their children young. She changed the subject. "I thought Dylan told me you had five children?"

"Yeah, the girls stayed at Grandma's last night. They'll be back a little bit later."

Joni transferred the stuffing from her mixing bowl to a casserole dish. She topped it with parsley and then replaced the lid.

"Have you sold any of your paintings?"

"Just a few at yard sales and the church bazaar, but I might have to sell some pretty soon. Richard's factory has them only working four days a week. We're scraping by, but just barely."

"I have a friend who has an art gallery in Cleveland. Want me to talk with him?"

"They aren't that good." Joni carried potatoes to the sink and picked up a paring knife. She turned back to Reggie, her face flushed.

Dylan strode up the steps and opened the kitchen door. "What's not good?"

"Joni's paintings. They're amazing." From the look on his face, Joni was right, Bobbie Jo hadn't gotten get the memo.

"Yeah, her paintings are terrific. I thought you were talking about her cooking not being any good. I was going to agree." He winked at Reggie. "Glad to see you're up."

His blue eyes twinkled as if he were happy to see her. He looked even more handsome than yesterday. His red plaid shirt had been replaced with a brightly colored Hawaiian style shirt, but he still wore jeans and boots. No baseball cap today..

"I thought I'd take Reggie on a tour of the town." He turned to his sister and playfully untied her apron strings.

"I don't know if it's a good idea. She's feeling a might sore this morning."

"Oh my—" He stared at her forehead, his mouth dropping open as he squinted, inspecting it. Apparently, her makeup hid it better than she thought.

"Don't say a word Dylan Monroe." Joni said in a threatening tone.

"Don't worry Reggie, it doesn't look too bad. At least it matches the purple flowers on my shirt." He ducked the oven mitt Joni sailed through the air at him.

"Well, it's a good thing. I would hate for the

fashion police in Fredericksburg to issue me a citation. I've had enough tickets for one week. A walk will do me good. I need to stretch out these sore muscles."

"The tour should take all of five minutes." Joni laughed.

"I can help here. I can't make a pie but I can wash dishes." Reggie's gaze focused on the disarray in the kitchen.

"I know it doesn't look like it at the moment, but I've got everything under control."

"Are you sure I can't help?"

"No." Joni shook her head. "Go stretch your muscles."

"Ready for the grand tour? Better get your coat. It's chilly out."

"Her coat's in the hall closet." Joni called out.

After helping her slide into her jacket, Dylan opened the door. Reggie stepped out and was greeted with a frost-covered yard.

They strolled down the tree-lined street. Leaves crunched beneath their feet. She breathed in deeply, smelling the smoke from nearby chimneys. She hadn't been far from the truth when she'd talked about a Norman Rockwell holiday.

She pulled her coat close and buttoned it.

Dylan pulled out a pack of gum and offered it to her. She shook her head and watched as he unwrapped two slices and popped them in his mouth.

"Have you lived here all your life, Dylan?"

"Pretty much. Except for my time in the Marines."

"What did you do in there?"

"A little of this and a little of that."

"You could be more specific."

Dylan smiled. "I could tell you, but then I'd have to kill you." He winked.

She shook her head and grimaced. "Such a tired old joke."

"Maybe, but—"

"Hey, Dylan." A voice called out.

Reggie turned towards the voice. A short, heavyset man stood in his garage waving. His thick fiery-red hair looked like a burning bush.

"Better go say hi to Mr. Matthews. He's a deacon at the church." They crossed to the other side of the street. "Hey, Mr. Matthews. Did Loraine kick you out of the house?"

"No way. I'm going to deep fry the turkey today. Just getting everything ready."

Reggie stared in awe at the man's garage. In spite of it being large enough for three cars, boxes filled every inch. A small path wound its way to the door leading into the house.

"You're not going to use that fryer in here, are you?" Worry lines furrowed into Dylan's forehead.

"Don't worry, Fireman Dylan." The man chuckled at his joke. "I know better than that."

"Fireman?" Reggie asked. "I thought you were a farmer."

"Didn't your beau tell you he's a fireman here in town? One of the best."

"He's not my—" She stopped. She hadn't ever said the word beau before in a real conversation. "We're just friends."

"Good thing. Bobbie Jo might have a thing or two to say." The man laughed and punched Dylan in the arm. "Just joshing you."

That name again. Who was this woman everyone seemed so worried about?

"This is Reggie." Dylan chuckled. "I'm taking her on a tour of the burg."

"That should really impress her." His bushy red eyebrows twitched like two squirrel tails as he laughed.

Reggie joined in. Apparently, everyone in Fredericksburg made fun of their little town.

"Didn't see you in church last night?" It came out as a question not a statement.

Reggie glanced over at Dylan to see his reaction to such a personal question, but Dylan just smiled and shrugged.

"You're right, you didn't. I was a little busy last night." Dylan winked at Reggie but didn't elaborate.

After saying their good-byes, they walked on, Dylan waved at a few more people and filled in the history on them. One was the bank president. Another had been a football quarterback in high school with a shot at the pros but hadn't made it because of a knee injury.

"Do you know everyone?"

"Just about. If I didn't grow up with them, I go to church with them or know them from the fire department or—"

"You didn't tell me you were a fireman."

"I said I did a little of this and a little of that."

"But still, you might have told me." Being a fireman was impressive.

They turned right at the end of the road and walked towards the center of town.

"Wouldn't you like to live in a bigger city? Somewhere with a little more excitement and where everyone doesn't know your personal business."

"Nope. I love it here. Why would I want to live someplace where nobody knows me?"

What would it be like living in a town where everyone knew everything about one? One's mistakes. One's failures. She shuddered at the thought. "You always hear how small towns are filled with gossips and busybodies. How everyone knows all your business."

"I suppose it's true in a way, but a good way."

"Sounds suffocating to me."

"Nah. They might get in your business now and then, but only because they care. I can tell you one thing, they're right there beside you when you need them. You can't find that in your big city."

7

Dylan continued playing the tour guide. The first highlight on the tour, was a square white building made of cinder blocks as they walked towards the center of the town.

"Now, this is our noodle factory. It used to be a car dealership but he moved to Apple Creek, so now it's the noodle factory."

They came to a small sign announcing a memorial park. The park consisted of a tiny thatch of grass and one bench. Below them a creek trickled by.

He pointed towards the edge of the creek. "There used to be houses here but they got washed away in the flood."

"Really. When?" Reggie asked, wondering about the families whose lives were destroyed by disaster.

"In 1969. Before my time, but one of the houses belonged to my uncle."

"Did he die?"

"No, but he lost everything. He had a huge collection of antique guns."

"He hunted?"

"No. Just collected guns."

"Do you hunt?" Reggie hated the thought of killing innocent animals.

"Not really. Now and then, I'll go out with some of my buddies, but I don't even bother carrying a gun with me anymore. I go out for the exercise."

She couldn't explain why, but it made her feel better.

He pointed out a donut shop that used to be a gas station and on the opposite side of the street, a pizza shop that once housed a gas station, as well. Opposite the pizza shop stood a library, formerly the town drugstore. He pointed out the only grocery store in town.

"What did that used to be?" Reggie asked with a smile.

"Just a grocery store. Always has been, as far as I know. Why do you ask?" He motioned at the four way stop with a flourish. "And this is the town square."

The square consisted of a flashing red light and four stop signs. Some tired looking plastic Christmas trees hung from the street lights. Her mind flashed to Cleveland's Public Square filled with monuments and surrounded by Terminal Tower, the Old Stone Church, and the elaborate decorations it now sported for the Christmas season.

Dylan might love this place, but she'd stick with big city life in spite of the fact she didn't know her neighbors' names.

"So, where's the gas station, now? Reggie asked.

"We don't have one."

"You don't have a gas station?" She stopped walking and stared open-mouthed at Dylan. She'd never been in a town without a gas station. "You've got to be kidding."

He shook his head.

"Where do you go to get gas?"

Before he could answer, an unfamiliar sound drew her attention to the road. Beating hooves. A horse and buggy rolled towards them. The buggy looked like a huge black box on wooden wheels. Mesmerized by the clacking and the clopping, Reggie gawked.

A man and woman, all in black, gave a friendly wave.

"Good morning," Dylan called.

After the buggy passed, two little heads popped up in the back window of the buggy. Both girls had on black bonnets, but their blond curls peeked through. The girls smiled and waved at Reggie. She waved back.

She'd seen the Amish portrayed on TV, but it hadn't seemed real.

"You don't need a gas station when you drive one of those. For the rest of us Englishers, we have to gas up before we get home."

"Englishers?"

"Yeah, it's what the Amish call us."

"Who were they?"

He shrugged. Don't know, they must be in town to visit some relatives."

"The Amish celebrate Thanksgiving?"

"Some do and some don't. Just depends on what their bishop decides."

"But they waved at us."

He chuckled and in an exaggerated southern accent said, "It's what we country folk do. It's called being friendly."

They walked a few more steps past a large modern hardware store. It looked out of place in the quaint little town. They sat down on a bench in front of the store.

"Did you know those people Richard talked about last night? The ones losing their farm."

"The Starks. Sure, I know them. Most of the farmers in the area know each other."

"Does it happen often? Losing farms."

"It happens. They've had a few bad years in a row, and then a few years ago he bought a new combine. I told him he could use ours, but he went out and bought one, anyway."

"Sounds awful." She stomped her feet to keep them warm.

"Well, we are at God's mercy concerning the weather, but there's a lot a farmer can do to make sure they don't get in a bad situation."

"I know farm land sells for a premium. Why not just sell the land, get rich, and retire somewhere warm?"

"Farming's not a job. It's our life. For most of us, these farms have been in our family for generations. It's not just something you sell because the going gets tough. We better get moving. The tour's almost finished." He held out a hand and she grasped it. He pulled her up, but kept her hand in his.

"What will happen to the Starks?"

"Some large corporation will probably buy them out. Maybe even let them stay and run the farm, but it won't ever be the same for them."

Dylan stopped in front of a small concrete

building. Bars covered the only window. Green block lettering above the door read JAIL.

"This is the old jail. I don't know when it was ever used as a jail but I guess it was at some time or another." He pointed at the road. "This is where the railroad tracks used to be but they were destroyed in the flood and the railroad never bothered to rebuild them. Now, we use it for a bike path." He pointed at a small brick building. "And here's the new fire station."

"When was it built?"

"Oh, I don't know. Probably in the 80s."

She arched an eyebrow at him and laughed. "And that's new?"

"It is around here."

She burrowed her hands deep into her coat pockets, wishing for gloves. The shivering made her sore muscles contract, which only caused more pain.

"The wind sure is picking up. Let's head back." Dylan said.

She nodded, not trusting herself to answer without teeth chattering. They walked in silence, until she finally built up the nerve to ask. "Who's this Bobbie Jo?" She regretted the words as soon as they escaped from her mouth. "Never mind. It's none of my business."

"I don't mind telling you. It's no big deal. It probably won't be the last time today you hear her name." Dylan put an arm around her shoulder, drawing Reggie close. The warmth felt good. "Bobbie Jo and I were best friends in school. Best friends, but nobody seems to understand that fact. Now that most of our friends are married and we're not, people keep thinking it's time for us to get hitched."

"And you don't agree?"

"We're buddies, and buddies don't get married." His arm slid from her shoulder and he took hold of her hand.

A warning bell went off in Reggie's head. She couldn't deny a certain spark, but Dylan wasn't dating material. She needed security, not the constant worry from one farming season to another. With regret, she pulled her hand back from his.

"Are you sure Bobbie Jo agrees with you? Joni seems to think you're wrong."

"Joni just wants to marry me off." He laughed. "She thinks people can't be happy without being married and having a house full of kids."

As they walked towards Joni's drive, a dark green mini-van pulled in and people tumbled out.

"Uncle Dylan." A little girl screamed and ran towards him.

Reggie estimated her age to be three or four. She wore a pink ball gown and a crown on top of her head. She also carried a royal scepter. He grabbed her up and twirled her around. Her crown fell off. Dylan set her back on the ground, picked up the crown and placed it back on her head.

She reached towards Dylan and he scooped her up. The little girl turned to Reggie, her cheeks rosy red from the laughing and twirling. Her blond hair stuck up in odd places under the crown. "Who are you?"

"I'm Reggie."

"I'm a princess," the child announced.

Joni, outside now, turned to Reggie. "We went to Disney World last summer and Missy has been wearing it ever since. My mother here encourages it."

"Life is hard enough. She deserves to be a princess for just as long as she wants." Joni's mother laughed. "Hi, I'm Mellie. I'm the mom." Her brown hair, with a generous sprinkling of gray, hung down her back in a neat braid. She wore a long blue jean skirt with a tie-dyed T-shirt and tennis shoes.

A man stepped from the other side of the van. He looked like Dylan, and he had striking blue eyes, as well. "I'm the dad, but most people call me Ken." He grasped Dylan's shoulder. "Where did you find this pretty little thing?"

"Let me tell you." Dylan put his arm around the older man's shoulder.

Before Dylan could tell his story, Missy interrupted the adults. "Are you going to marry my Uncle Dylan?"

That brought hoots and cheers to the crowd gathered by the van. Dylan's dad laughed and punched his son's arm. "He could only be so lucky."

The group went into the house. As the morning wore on, more people arrived. Dylan introduced her to aunts, uncles, and his grandmother. The house seemed dwarfed as it filled up with adults and children. The day stretched into a blur of activity, laughter, and love—a far cry from Reggie's usual holiday routine. Hers normally consisted of watching TV, cooking pasta, and if she could find an open store, some shopping.

When Joni announced dinner, the group gathered in the formal dining room. The table stretched the full length of the room. A quick count of the chairs showed nineteen. Two turkeys and a ham, along with all the trimmings, loaded the table.

After everyone was seated, Ken stood and prayed. Uncomfortable, Reggie bowed her head in respect for their traditions. She had nothing against God, or religion, but it wasn't part of her life.

People talked and laughed and passed food. Dylan's family went out of their way to make her feel comfortable. Surprised, she found herself having a good time.

After the meal, the men left the table and went into the living room to watch football on the big screen TV. The children ran off in different directions, some outside, some to the basement, and some to the bedrooms. The women stayed behind. Several stood and began to clean off the table.

"I promised to stop over at Bobbie Jo's parents for a few minutes for dessert. Want to come with me?" Dylan leaned over to Reggie.

"Maybe, I shouldn't."

"Nonsense. It'll be fine."

She had to meet this woman whom he claimed was his best friend.

8

Early Friday morning, they walked up the sidewalk towards Reggie's condo. A light sprinkling of snow had fallen during the night, making the half-bare trees look even more forlorn.

The parking lot was full of cars and not one person to be seen. Dylan glanced around the condo grounds and was struck by the differences in their lives. But in spite of those differences, he found himself attracted to Reggie.

Not that anything would come of it. Not only did they live too far apart, but the distance in their lifestyles was even greater. A big city lawyer and a simple country farmer and fireman just didn't mesh.

Dylan glanced over at Reggie. Her spine was straight, as if steeling herself for what lay ahead. Gorgeous and tough. To be abandoned by her parents had to be devastating, and yet she'd succeeded in becoming a lawyer.

"Don't worry. I'm not going to fall apart this time." She gave him a resolute smile as she juggled several bags of cleaning supplies.

"I didn't think you would. It won't be so bad with two of us working." Dylan reassured her. "We'll be done before you know it."

"You hardly know me and yet you've done so

much. Now you're insisting on helping me clean up my trashed apartment. Why?"

"It's my slow season at the farm so I've got nothing better to do." There was no logical way to explain the protectiveness he felt for her.

"Good answer, now tell me the real reason." She set her bags on the steps and slid her key into the lock. She opened the door and led the way.

It looked worse than Dylan remembered.

"Yep, it's still a disaster." Her face held no expression.

"Time to get busy." Dylan held up the cleaning supplies .

"I just can't believe Trent did this to me." Shaking her head, Reggie gazed around her apartment.

He'd sure like to have a little chat with this loser. Reggie should have reported the vandalism, but he wouldn't bring it up again.

"Let's start with the stuff to be thrown out, first." He forced his voice to sound cheerful. "That will be half the battle, don't you think?"

"We're not doing anything until you answer my question." Reggie put hands on her hips, and her green eyes twinkled as she stared at Dylan.

"What question?"

"Why…why are you being so nice to me?" Reggie obviously wasn't used to people doing things for her without wanting something back.

"Two reasons." Dylan turned on his most charming smile. "First, you've grown on me. Kinda like a ripe tomato in June. That's what I'm telling all my buddies."

"A tomato? Being compared to a vegetable

isn't particularly flattering."

"Well it is if you love tomatoes as much as I do." He laughed. "And besides tomatoes don't usually get ripe until July so tomatoes in June are a beauty to behold—and they are a fruit, which is much more appealing than a vegetable, don't you think?"

"I know I'm going to regret this, but what's the other one?"

"We..ell," he said, drawing the word out so it became two syllables. "The other reason is the golden rule. You know do unto others…"

"Sounds good on paper, but people don't really do that." She arched an eyebrow.

"Reggie, there are good people out there who do care about other people. I know you have a hard time trusting people. I hope you know you can trust me."

"And you follow this rule all the time?" Her eyes widened and her mouth moved.

"Can't say I do but I try. Jesus told us to love our enemies, not that you're my enemy—even if you did crash into me."

"And here I thought it was because you were—" A knock stopped her words mid-sentence. Reggie walked over to answer it. "Trent, what are you doing here?"

"I thought you might want your key back." A man pushed past Reggie without an invitation, and held up a key. He stared at the room, mouth agape, shocked by the condition of the apartment.

"Whoa! What happened here?"

"As if you didn't know, Trent."

Dylan saw the smirk. Trent's shock was as

bogus as a three dollar bill. Reggie was right to kick this loser to the curb.

"I don't know what you're talking about, Reg." His voice whined like a race car hitting a curve.

His gaze locked on Dylan. Trent's face turned red and he threw the key on the floor. It landed in a cloud of stuffing from the couch.

A thick forelock of bluish-black hair fell forward onto his perfectly chiseled face. A smartly-dressed man, complete with green work slacks and a matching polo shirt.

"Is this the...well I wouldn't call him a man because men don't hurt women." Dylan stepped forward and stood by Reggie. "Is this the guy who trashed your apartment, Reggie?"

"Stick a boot in it, dude." He turned to Reggie. "Is this who you dumped me for? From the look of the bruise on your forehead you must have lost your mind." Trent glared at Dylan.

"I'll tell you—"

Reggie laid a hand on Dylan's arm. "Trent, you need to leave. Get out and don't ever call me again. If you do, you'll—"

"You're letting this dude accuse me of this? I can't believe it." Trent whined. "I've got better things to do with my time. And who's this guy, anyway? Your new lover? You sure work fast. I knew what kind of woman you were, but—"

"Hey, I think that's enough." Dylan stepped towards Trent, fists clenched at his side. *Forgive me, Lord, but...* "You'd best leave while you can still walk. You just insulted this lady."

"Who do you think you are?" Trent turned

and gave Dylan a scathing look. He turned towards Reggie. "I want to talk to you alone, Reg. Let's go outside."

"I'm a little busy at the moment. Maybe you'd like to stay and help us." Reggie gave him a disgusted look. "Just get out of here and leave me alone."

Trent grabbed Reggie's arm and pulled her towards the door. Sarcasm dripped from his mouth. "Come on, sweetie. I need to talk to you. Alone."

This wasn't going to happen in front of him. Dylan took three quick steps and blocked the doorway. "Let go of her, now."

Reggie twisted away but Trent's grip remained firm.

"This has nothing to do with—" Trent shoved Dylan with his free hand.

Dylan grabbed Trent by his shirt, backing him up against the wall. Trent had released Reggie somewhere along the way, and Dylan heard Reggie call his name, but he ignored her. Trent needed a lesson in treating women with respect.

With his face inches from Trent's, Dylan held the man. "It's not OK to put your hands on a woman, ever. She told you to leave her alone and that's what you need to do. Got it?" He enunciated each word slowly and clearly, as if speaking to a five-year-old.

Trent's face turned red then white. His hand came up and attempted to dislodge Dylan from his shirt, but failed.

"I don't know who you think you—" The words came out as a whine.

"The name's Dylan Monroe. I'm in the phone book, if you want to look me up sometime. Want me to spell it for you?"

"Let go of me."

"I'd better not hear of you bothering Reggie again. Or you'll hear from me and you aren't going to like it." Dylan let go of Trent's shirt.

Trent opened his mouth, but snapped it shut as Dylan leaned towards him. Stomping towards the door, he whirled around and glared at Dylan, then pointed his finger at Reggie.

"This isn't over."

"Yes, Trent, it is." Reggie said firmly.

9

Reggie and Dylan stared at the door for a moment and then Dylan turned to her. "Was it something I said?"

Shaking, Reggie sat down on the nearest chair, slashed up cushion and all. She took a deep breath.

"Are you OK?" Dylan walked over and patted her shoulder.

She let out her breath and nodded.

"Prince Charming, huh?" Dylan asked, as he unwrapped a slice of gum.

"What can I say? I don't make the best choices when it comes to picking men."

"Forget about it," Dylan said in his best imitation of a Brooklyn tough guy. He walked over to the cleaning supplies now on the floor. He tossed her a box of trash bags and kept one for himself. "Let's get busy. I'll take the kitchen and you take this room."

"But the kitchen's the worst..."

Dylan started whistling and waved. In reality, his blood boiled. The man trashed Reggie's apartment, then came over to rub salt into the wound. He'd probably been hanging around for the past two days waiting for her. Not a nice guy.

Beautiful, smart, funny, and successful, what

would make her pick a man like Trent? Reggie deserved to be treated like a princess.

In the kitchen, he picked up the broken dishes and quickly moved on to the floor. He scooped the mess up and threw it in a trash bag. He applied cleaner to the dried goo, then headed through the living room to set the full trash bag outside the door. He would put them in his truck later. No reason for them to sit here until her next trash pickup. Reggie's eyes were red, and she wiped away tears.

He walked outside and set the trash bag down. He came back in, struck a pose and then went into a rendition of Elvis and Jailhouse Rock, gyrating hips and all.

Reggie's mouth dropped open in surprise but her gaze lit up.

He added in some new dance moves.

By the end of the song, Reggie was holding her sides, laughing.

He bowed. "Thank you, Thank you, very much. Hi-Ho-Hi-Ho, off to the kitchen I go," he sang as he marched off.

Fifteen minutes later, he walked back through the living room with a trash bag in each hand. Reggie took out a bag of trash as well. She held the door open for him.

They stood outside breathing in the fresh crisp air. In spite of the cold, he suggested they open some windows to air out Reggie's apartment.

"The kitchen's done, except for a good scrubbing." Dylan told her.

"The living room's done, except I have to clean up the figurines." Her voice shook with emotion.

Dylan nodded sympathetically even though he didn't exactly know why the figurines were important to Reggie. A collection of some kind? His sister had something like that, too.

"I can't believe he broke them." Her eyes filled with tears and her lips quivered. "He knew how important they were to me. I've been collecting them since high school graduation. My foster mother gave me my first one. From then on, I saved my pennies and nickels so I could buy one for my birthday and Christmas. Most of the time, it was the only gift I'd get."

She bit her lip and looked up at the sky for a moment. Her eyes held unshed tears when she looked back at Dylan. His heart broke for her. He stepped close and wrapped his arms around her. Leaning down, his face grazed her hair. The scent of peaches greeted him.

He fought the urge to kiss her. Reggie needed a friend. Taking a deep breath, he stepped away. "I'll clean up the figurines. You start on the bedroom. We'll be done by the time we need to go pick up your rental car."

"I don't know how to repay you." Reggie wiped away a tear.

"We've already been—"

Shots rang out from the woods to their left. Dust flew up several feet from them. Reggie looked around, as if she didn't recognize the sound, but without a moment's hesitation, he threw himself against her and they both fell to the ground. More shots. He rolled her towards the house.

"Someone's shooting. Quick, crawl into the house." Dylan ordered. He lifted himself up and she scooted underneath him. As she crawled, he crab walked behind her in such a way to keep his body covering hers. Once in the house, he slammed the door just as more shots rang out. The door shook from the impact of the bullets. Dylan reached up and locked it.

Reggie started to stand up.

"No, stay down and get behind the kitchen island." He told her.

She did so without arguing, while Dylan pulled out his cell and dialed 911. After the phone call, he went to Reggie. She huddled behind the kitchen island sobbing. The toughness was gone. He wrapped his arms around her.

"I have to go outside." His Marine training kicked in. He needed to defuse this situation before someone got hurt.

"You can't go outside. Someone shot at us." Panic tinged her voice. She clutched his arms tighter.

"I have to or he'll get away."

"No. He'll kill you." She grabbed him.

"Nah, he won't shoot me. He's trying to scare you."

"You act as if you know who's shooting at us."

"I do. It's Trent. He told you he'd make you pay."

"Trent? I don't think he even owns a gun, much less know how to shoot one." Open-mouthed, she stared at Dylan. "Trent would never do something like this."

"I'm going out the back way and circle around. You lock the door after I leave and don't open it unless it's me, or the police." He patted her hands in reassurance. "I'll be fine. Don't worry."

Sirens wailed in the distance.

"Good, the cops will be here in any moment. Now you don't have to go outside."

"You're right. The sirens probably chased him off." He waited a few seconds, listening, then held out a hand and helped her up. As she stood, he pulled her to him. She nuzzled in close. He caressed her hair. He'd never be able to eat a peach again without thinking of her.

She stepped away, but stayed in his embrace. "I don't know what I would have done if you hadn't been here. You make me feel safe."

He leaned down and brushed his lips against her cheek. Her arms went around him, making his heart beat a little faster. He focused in on her lips and leaned closer.

The jarring of the doorbell caused them to jump away from each other.

"You'd think we were a couple of school kids or something." Dylan laughed. "I'll get the door."

Two officers stood outside staring at the bullet holes as Dylan opened the door. One looked up at Dylan. "I guess the caller was right when they said someone was shooting at them."

"The shots came from over there. We couldn't see but I have a pretty good idea who it was." Dylan said, pointing at the trees.

"Let's back up a minute. I'm Officer Pettry and this is my partner Officer Montgomery and you are?"

"I'm Dylan Monroe and this is Reggie Meyers. It's her apartment. Come on inside."

"What happened in here?" Officer Pettry's gaze went to the broken figurines still on the floor and the shredded sofa, then back at Dylan with suspicion.

Reggie stepped forward and took charge.

"Sounds like the ex-boyfriend to me." Officer Pettry listened, then nodded.

"I don't believe Trent shot at us. He doesn't even own a gun. It couldn't have been him." Her voice sounded as if she were Trent's lawyer. Why did she keep defending the creep?

"I agree with my partner. It's the ex." Officer Montgomery looked at Dylan.

"Aren't you listening? I'm sure Trent did this." She was getting more irritated and gestured at the apartment. "But I'm telling you, he didn't shoot at us. Probably just some kids playing a prank."

"Some prank." Montgomery said.

"Are you trying to tell me the two incidents aren't related to each other?" Pettry looked at Reggie, his tone snide.

"That's exactly what I'm saying." Reggie refused to back down.

"A lot of drama for one woman." Officer Pettry said. "What are you doing to make everyone mad at you?"

"Give us your boyfriend's name, phone number, and address." Officer Montgomery pulled out a tablet from his pocket.

"I already told—"

"We'll have to talk to him about the incident.

Do you want to press charges for trashing your apartment?"

"No." Reggie's face turned red and her gaze fell to the floor.

"Then we'll go check around and see if we can collect evidence." Officer Montgomery put away his pen and notebook. "We may return later today, if something comes up."

10

Reggie was tempted to curl up in a ball, but she forced away the negative thoughts. Dwelling on the bad never helped.

Dylan sat in the slashed up easy chair while she parked herself on the cushionless sofa. "I guess you're still in love with him, huh?" Dylan eyed her, his voice distant.

"I'm not in love with him, and never was. He was so sweet at first, but the longer we dated the nastier he became. It's why I broke up with him. He has this wild idea I left him for someone else, but the truth of the matter is…" She hated to admit it. It made her feel weak, powerless. Biting her lip, she looked at Dylan. "The truth of the matter is, he scared me when he'd lose his temper." She got up. "I need to check my sugar level."

Dylan followed her to the kitchen and leaned against the counter as Reggie pricked her finger and smeared the drop of blood on the testing strip. She placed the strip in the meter and waited for the numbers to pop up on the screen.

"Does it hurt?"

"Not really. I don't even think about it."

"How long have you been diabetic?"

She shrugged and opened the refrigerator,

grateful Dylan had thought to bring food with them. "Since I was born as far as I know. I guess Mom didn't want the bother of a sick child. Who could blame her?"

"Do you consider yourself sick?" Dylan asked.

"Not really. But it is something I hate. It was one of the reasons foster homes kept sending me back. I felt like a freak, like I had a contagious disease and if they touched me they would catch it." The question surprised Reggie. She pulled out the cheese and meat from the refrigerator.

"I'm really sorry you had to go through all that." He came up behind her and touched her hair.

"It's just a condition I have to manage. I'm no more sick than someone with asthma. I'm stronger and healthier than a lot of people." Her breath caught in her throat. She wanted to let him hold her, comfort her, take her hurt away. *I can't do that. It wouldn't be fair to send him mixed signals.* Reggie carried the snack to her round dinette table and set it down, then went back for silverware. "Time to eat."

"I know you're going to love this bologna." He held up the ring of brown lunch meat. It reminded her of summer sausage. "The only place it's made is a small town called Trail south of Fredericksburg." Dylan opened the freezer and gave her a now-chilled bottle of water.

"Looks a little spicy for my taste."

He sliced a piece off and handed it to her, then continued cutting more.

"Mmm. Not bad." She reached for another piece.

"I told you. Too bad I forgot to buy mustard. Spicy mustard goes great with it. Try it with the Swiss cheese."

Dylan entertained her with family stories as they ate. When they were finished, he stood. "Time to get back to work."

"I guess I'll mop." Reggie groaned inwardly, but it had to be done.

An hour later, they both threw themselves down in tattered chairs in the living room. The only thing left was to vacuum.

"I sure love spending time with you, but I'm glad we're finished." Dylan said.

"I don't know how to thank you. There's no way I could have done it by myself. I would have given up and gone to bed."

"*Pshaw*. It was nothing and I doubt very much if you would have gone to bed. I have a pretty good idea you're a lot tougher than you feel right now."

She shrugged. The past few days with Dylan had been wonderful. He anticipated her every need. Sweet and kind and helpful. A person could get use to this kind of treatment.

She smiled at him. Her heart gave a flutter as he smiled back at her through half-closed eyes. *Stop it. It would never work.* Just because he was a hunk and sweet as could be didn't make him dating material. Besides, she could never be comfortable wondering if he might lose the farm and livelihood like the Starks.

"What are you going to do now?"

"What do you mean?" For one uncomfortable moment, it was as if he'd known her thoughts.

"You can't stay here tonight."

His question almost brought on the tears once again. She'd better toughen up or she'd never become the great lawyer she planned to be. "I am not leaving my home."

"Those weren't BBs in the door."

"I know." She held up a hand. "But what am I supposed to do? I can't just run away. This is my home."

"Don't you have any friends you can stay with for a few days until the cops figure this out?"

Before Reggie could answer, her phone rang. As she walked to the phone, the doorbell rang. She looked back and forth.

"You take the phone. I'll answer the door." Dylan said.

She nodded.

****

After glancing through the peep hole, Dylan opened the door.

Officers Pettry and Montgomery were grim-faced. A woman stood with them.

He motioned them to come in.

Reggie's voice filled the tiny apartment, her ear pressed against the receiver. "Look, Trent. I didn't tell them you shot at me. In fact, I told them the opposite. But after the mess you made in my apartment, you became the most likely suspect. Nothing I could do about it. It's your own fault."

Dylan watched her take a deep breath. In a flash, he saw her strength reappear. She stood straighter and her shoulders went back. Right before his eyes, she transformed from victim to attorney.

"Trent." Her voice was iron strong. "Do not call me again. Monday morning, I will get a restraining order. I'm sure with the reports of the police standing in my living room at this very moment, it won't be a problem. And if I even see your shadow, I'll call the cops. You got it?"

Dylan heard Trent yelling as Reggie quietly replaced the receiver. She looked at the group. "Trent."

Dylan felt like clapping.

The other woman had a tired face framed by a short bob, sprinkled with gray. She was dressed in Levi's and tennis shoes with a brown corduroy jacket. The overall impression spoke of casual professional. "I'm Detective Cindy Sellers." She fished a badge from her pocket and showed it to Reggie. "I've been assigned to your case, Ms. Meyers."

"You talked with Trent, from what he told me between the ranting."

"Yes." The woman stared at Reggie as if assessing her state of mind.

Dylan sensed the next words were not going to be comforting by the look on the detective's face.

"Trent didn't do the shooting. The bar where he drinks happens to have a surveillance camera. The video shows him at the bar before, during, and after the shooting." Her graveled words were short and clipped. Holding her pen like a cigarette she tapped the notebook in an anxious beat. Deep lines grew vertically from her upper lip.

Dylan recognized a fellow smoker and offered her slice of gum.

"I never believed he did, but he vandalized my apartment. He admitted it to me on the phone."

"He admitted it to us as well. Do you want to press charges?"

"I just want him to leave me alone. If I press charges it will prolong our relationship, and I want it to be over."

"If he bothers you anymore, call me." The detective leaned close to Reggie. "Sometimes, the only solution is to press charges. He was pretty shook up when I talked with him. I don't think he's going to bother you anymore."

"We need to find the shooter before he tries it again." Dylan followed them into the living room.

"What makes you think Reggie was the target? Could have been you?" Detective Sellers looked at Dylan.

"If I had been the target, they would have shot at me while we were at my house, not hers. This is only the second time I've been here." He joined the other officers leaning against the wall. "And besides, I'm one of the good guys." He pointed at Reggie. "Just ask her."

Reggie rolled her eyes. "He does appear to be one of the good guys, but I'm reserving judgment."

"Whoever it was, they weren't playing around. They used a .357 Magnum." Detective Sellers looked back and forth between the two of them.

Dylan whistled. "You're right. That's a pretty

large caliber, meant to do serious damage. What are you advising Reggie to do? Is it safe for her to stay here or what?"

"Let me put it this way. If she were my girlfriend, she wouldn't be staying here."

"You heard the man, but it's up to you." Dylan looked at Reggie.

"I know. I know." Frustration seeped in her voice. "I'll call a friend."

"We have a few more questions before you leave and we'll need a number to reach you at." Detective Sellers told her.

"Of course. Sit down." Reggie gestured at her ruined furniture. "Most of the stuffing's out of it but it's better than standing up."

"Actually, several of your neighbors weren't home before, so we're going to interview them while Detective Sellers talks with you. We might get lucky. Someone might have seen something or noticed an odd person on a different day."

After Montgomery and Pettry left, Cindy took a tape recorder from her pocket and held it up. "Is it OK with you if we record this?"

"I don't mind at all. Just let me get mine and we can both record it."

Dylan hid his smile. The tough lady lawyer was back.

"Why do you want to do that, Ms. Meyers?" Detective Sellers sounded perplexed

"For the same reason you do, Detective Sellers." Reggie walked out of the room and returned with her mini-recorder. After setting it on the coffee table, and each recording Reggie's consent for both the interview and Dylan's presence, the questions began.

"Who do you work for, Ms. Meyers?"

"I'm an apprentice for a law firm, Benton and Greene. I mostly work with contracts and I've assisted on a few criminal cases."

"I'm going to need copies of those cases. Did any case stand out to you? Maybe an angry client?" The detective opened up a container of mints, offered them to the others, then popped several in her mouth.

"None come to mind at the moment. No one angry enough to shoot at me."

Dylan wanted to wrap her in his arms. She looked so small curled on the sofa, her doe-like eyes tired from worry.

"Keep thinking about it. You've made somebody unhappy."

"Unhappy enough to want to kill me?" Reggie shook her head. "This whole thing is so bizarre."

"What about your family?" Detective Sellers adjusted the volume on the recorder and pushed it closer to Reggie.

Reggie took a deep breath.

Dylan grimaced, feeling bad she had to tell it again. He couldn't imagine life without his parents.

"No parents. I grew up in the foster system in Pennsylvania."

"Oh, sorry." The detective looked up from the notes she was taking.

"It sounds worse than it was." Reggie looked over at Dylan. "I was doing OK until a few days ago. Now, my life appears to be falling apart."

The doorbell rang again. Dylan answered it.

A tall woman with curly brown hair and glasses stood on the threshold.

"Alexis. I was going to call you." Reggie jumped up and went to the woman.

Alexis scanned the room, seeing Dylan, the detective taking notes, the recorders, and the slashed up sofa and chairs. Her eyes grew wide. "What is going on? I've been trying to call you all day."

"I've been a little busy." Reggie gestured at her ruined apartment.

11

"Unbelievable."

It was the fourth or fifth time Reggie's friend said the word.

A thick fog of emotions hung in the air. Reggie and Alexis sat on the sofa clinging to each other and wiping away tears. Female bonding at its best was happening on the shredded couch.

He stood at a safe distance as the atmosphere in the room screamed no-men-allowed. *I can keep her safe—if only she lets me.*

The detective gathered her notes and recorder. "I'm done for now. I've got your phone number. Have you decided where you'll stay?"

"Of course, she can stay with me." Alexis offered. She looked at the detective. "I live at The Park Condos."

"Good idea." Detective Sellers beamed her approval. "I think it would be a safe place for you, Reggie. You should take her up on the invitation."

After the detective left, Alexis's gaze raked over Dylan. "And who are you?"

"I'm Dylan Monroe." Dylan locked the door and turned back towards Alexis.

Before he could say more, Reggie took control. "Alexis!" Reggie elbowed her in the ribs. "I think you need to help me pack a few things." She gave a little self-conscious laugh.

They moved to the bedroom. Dylan stared after them. *Women.* Almost thirty, and he still didn't understand them, but it *was* nice to hear Reggie laugh.

He paced like a caged tiger. They needed to hurry. It was growing darker outside, and the shooter could still be around, although with the presence of the police cars, still in the parking lot, he doubted it.

Loud scraping against the hardwood floor filled the hallway, as they returned with two heavy suitcases.

"You can't walk out the door with that monster suitcase." Dylan threw up his hands in frustration. "He could be watching us."

It was painful to see the happiness drain from Reggie's face. But he had no choice. Her life depended on it.

Alexis took baby steps towards Dylan. "By the way, I'm Alexis Krinkle." Her hand shook as she placed it in Dylan's. "I'm Reggie's secretary, but we don't use that word any longer. Not PC, you know."

"That's fantastic. While we work on getting out of here, can you think of a case that turned sour?" *Please Lord, give me wisdom to help Reggie.* Dylan looked at his watch. He moved the curtain to peek outside.

It was dark. Across the parking lot stood apartment B. It contained a checker board of windows. Most were black, except a few yellow-lit squares behind closed curtains. The parking lot almost empty, the police cars now gone.

"Alexis, perhaps you should go back to your

condo and I'll bring Reggie later."

"Sounds like a plan."

"And you'll need to take some time off work until the police find out what's going on." Dylan added softly, knowing his words wouldn't make her happy.

"No way." Reggie crossed her arms. "I am not going to let some crazy person keep me from doing my job. I refuse to let them scare me."

"Reggie, be reasonable. You don't want to make—" Alexis looked shocked.

"I am being reasonable. I *am* going to work on Monday." Reggie's chin went up and her shoulders went back. Her fighting stance.

"That's crazy Reggie, have you lost all your senses!" Alexis stood inches from Reggie.

"OK, if we don't get outa here soon, we won't need to worry about working Monday or any day." Dylan said forcefully.

Both women turned to stare at him, shocked.

Oh, great. His big mouth had upset them. He needed to learn to be more tactful, but being tactful wasn't on his mind at the moment. Reggie's safety was. "Reggie, be reasonable. Let's stick with the plan to go to Alexis's for the time being. We'll worry about work later. I'll take you to pick up the rental car, and then you can drive to Alexis's place. Deal?"

Her emerald eyes filled with tears and she bit her lip, making her look vulnerable and sexy at the same time. She nodded.

"Good. I'll come back here after you get the rental to pick up your stuff and I'll bring it to you later." *After I make sure I'm not followed.*

12

Dylan drove through the holiday weekend rush hour towards Reggie's condo.

Hard to believe the gun shots didn't involve Trent. Even if the loser had a solid alibi, it didn't mean he wasn't involved in the shooting. Trent wouldn't be the first person to hire a hit man.

Logic told him to walk away, but his conscience wouldn't let him. He didn't know Reggie well, but his instincts told him she was a good person.

If someone had helped his sister, she might still be alive. Reggie needed help, and he was determined to give it to her.

He pulled back into the apartment's parking lot. Reggie had her rental car and was safely on her way to Alexis's condo. Pretending to be talking on his cell phone, he assessed the situation. When he was sure no one laid in wait, he hopped out of the truck and jogged to her apartment.

Reggie's things still sat by the chair. He couldn't carry them out in a suitcase. It would be like taking out a billboard announcing Reggie had left her apartment.

He thought for a moment. He could put her things in garbage bags to camouflage them. Hopefully, it would be enough to throw anyone off who might be watching.

He saw Reggie's vacuum. It was the only thing they hadn't finished. Might as well do it before he left. As he vacuumed, a stray piece of a porcelain caught his eye, half hidden under the end table. As he bent down to pick it up, he glanced at the bottom side of the end table, and saw a small, round plastic case with a red flashing light.

Although surprised, it was not the first time he'd seen one. In fact, he'd installed them more than once. Someone had bugged Reggie's apartment.

His mind played back their conversations. They'd heard every word uttered in the apartment, including where Reggie was.

He grabbed his cell phone, but then realized he didn't have Alexis's or Reggie's number. He didn't have the detective's number, either. He picked up the garbage bags with Reggie's things, and double-timed to his truck.

He jumped in and sped off.

****

Reggie pretended to relax as she stretched out on Alexis's couch, but her mind refused to obey. She kept reliving the moments the shots rang out and Dylan had pushed her to the ground, protecting her with his own body. He'd risked his life to save hers. Tears filled her eyes. No one had ever done such a thing for her and she hadn't even thanked him.

At least she felt some semblance of safety here

with Alexis. It was the first time since being shot at she hadn't felt the need to look over her shoulder every fifteen seconds. Being on the eighth floor helped.

Alexis sang an old rock and roll song as she cooked them an early dinner. Giving up the façade of relaxing, Reggie walked to the kitchen.

This kitchen was convenient, if nothing else. All Alexis had to do was turn from one direction to the other to reach the refrigerator, the cupboards or the stove. It was perfect unless the cook was claustrophobic.

"Can I help?"

"I thought you were resting," her friend said.

"No such luck. I kept replaying Dylan pushing me to the ground after we heard the shots. Do you realize he saved my life?"

"I guess you're right. I didn't think about it. He's quite the guy." Alexis stopped chopping the tomatoes for the salad and stared at Reggie.

"He's a farmer."

"And what's wrong with that?"

"Nothing, I supp—"

Fire alarms from the hall drowned out the rest of her sentence. Reggie and Alexis stared at each other, neither moving.

"What is going on?" Alexis yelled loud enough to be heard over the clanging of the alarms. She dropped her knife and snatched the phone from its base. She hit the numbers for the condo office and waited.

"No answer. Might be the real thing. We better leave." Alexis's eyes darted around the room. "Where's my purse?" Spying it, she rushed over, grabbed it and urged Reggie to hurry.

Reggie grabbed her own bag and jogged to the door. She hated the thought of being outside again. It made her feel vulnerable. She could still remember the sound of the shots. She stopped moving. How likely was it that someone would shoot at her, and Alexis's apartment complex would have a fire on the same day? Not very. It seemed too farfetched.

Alexis's hand moved towards the knob.

"Don't open it, Alexis," Reggie screamed.

****

Please God, keep her safe.

Dylan pulled into condo's parking lot, a knot in his stomach. People streamed out of the building. Police, fire, and emergency vehicles crowded the parking lot. Sirens split the afternoon air.

He was too late.

****

Alexis turned towards Reggie, her face filled with confusion.

"Maybe, we shouldn't go out. It could be a trick. After all, someone did shoot at me today."

"But I smell smoke. Don't you smell it?" Alexis's eyes grew wide.

"Look through the peephole." Reggie pointed at the door.

"The hall is filled with smoke and people are running down the hall. We need to get out, too.

We can't stay here." Alexis pointed at the smoke seeping under the door.

Reggie took several steps away from the door. "I'm not going out there. Something feels wrong. You go. I'm staying here. I'll open your patio door for fresh air. I'll be fine."

"This is crazy, Reggie. You can't stay in here if the building's on fire."

****

Dylan stared at the green fire engines. Whoever bugged Reggie's place had beaten him here. It was the only explanation.

He jumped out of the car and rushed towards the building. He scanned the crowd. No Reggie. No Alexis.

A woman stood nearby clutching a baby in her arms.

"What's going on?" he asked, touching her shoulder.

"Fire." The woman said as she wiped tears away. "Smoke was everywhere."

"You don't happen to know Alexis Krinkle?"

She shook her head.

"Thanks." Dylan called back as he headed towards the door. His gaze darted from person to person, searching the faces. His mind shuffled through the options the would-be killer had. He could wait outside and shoot Reggie when she came out, or knock on Alexis's door as a concerned neighbor and then attack.

Think. Think. Which would he do if he wanted to kill someone?

God give me wisdom.

Too many risks to wait until Reggie came outside. With all the people milling about in the semi-darkness, he could shoot the wrong person, could be seen, possibly even stopped by some do-gooder. And police and fireman were everywhere.

But if he stood outside Alexis's door and waited for them to come out, he could take care of the problem easy enough. Then just walk away through the crowd with no one being the wiser.

Dylan rushed towards the main entrance, clogged with a sea of humanity. He pushed his way forward. A fireman and a policeman stood by the door directing and calming the frightened residents.

As Dylan approached the door, the policeman stepped forward. "You can't go inside, sir."

"I have to. I think…" Dylan knew the officer would be skeptical-very skeptical. He took a deep breath. *Please God, help me out here.* "I know it sounds crazy, but I think someone is trying to kill two friends who are inside the building."

"What are you talking about?" The cop's eyes grew wide with surprise and then suspicion.

"You can check with the police. Someone already shot at her once today. I think this is a ruse to get to her. I've got to get in there."

"What's the news on the fire?" The policeman studied Dylan for a moment and then turned back to the fireman.

"Prank. Just a bunch of smoke bombs."

He knew it. The perfect cover to get in and out of the building. The shooter had no doubt been waiting for Reggie at Alexis's door. As soon as the women opened the door to leave, Reggie would be an easy target. He refused to let his mind go any further. He had to get up to them. Either, or both women could be hurt.

"What floor?" Dylan asked.

"Several floors, the tenth, the ninth, and the eighth." The fireman told him.

"My friend lives on the eighth." Dylan told the officer. "Apartment 8217."

Understanding dawned in the officer's eyes. "You stay. I'll go. What was the number again?"

Dylan repeated it and added, "I'm coming with you."

The policeman didn't stop him. "The elevators are stopped. Have to take the stairs." The policeman called, as he ran towards the stairwell's door.

People still trudged down. Dylan quickly passed the officer and kept running. At the eighth floor, he stopped to catch his breath. He needed to be calm. He opened the door and walked through.

A wall of smoke and the clanging of alarms greeted him. Letting his military training take over, Dylan looked both ways. Smoke burned his eyes, nose, and throat, and clouded his vision, but he scanned apartment numbers until he figured out which way Alexis's condo should be.

The clanging of the fire alarms silenced his movement as he crept through the smoke filled hallway. Breathing in the smoke, he resisted the urge to cough. He lifted the tail of his shirt and held it over his nose for a few seconds.

The chemical fog should be dissipating soon, if it really was a smoke bomb. As he got closer, he heard a voice yelling.

"Hey, open up. There's a fire in the building. I know you're in there. I saw you go in. We gotta get out. Hurry up."

Please God, don't let Alexis open the door. Smoke-induced tears blurred his vision. He forced down a cough and crept along the wall.

Almost there. Just a few more steps. His eyes focused on the silhouette of the gun pointed at the door.

Dylan leaped through the air just as the man turned towards him. He looked down the dark tunnel of a gun barrel as a huge explosion reverberated in the hallway. He could feel the heated breath of the bullet as it whizzed a path through the air, just missing his cheek.

Both men hit the floor with Dylan on top.

"Stay in the apartment." He yelled, loud enough to be heard over the clanging of the fire alarm.

"Dylan, is that you?" Alexis called.

They wrestled for the gun that slid away. Grunting and swearing, the gunman outweighed Dylan by fifty pounds. If Dylan didn't get to the gun first, he was a dead man. Reggie's face flashed before him, renewing his strength.

A .357 magnum. A cold, gleaming-steel puppet waiting for the marionette to give the killing order. Both men reached out with fingers spread, towards the weapon. The gunman broke free and grasped at the gun, but Dylan was quicker. He grabbed the man's arm and bent it backwards.

"Police." A voice down the hall yelled.

Movement from behind and then, someone hit his head—hard. *There were two men?* He barely had time to digest that when the pain hit.

Losing his balance, Dylan fell to the floor as both men bolted down the hallway, disappearing like ghosts into the smoke.

13

The scent of smoke lingered in the apartment.

Reggie sat beside Dylan on the couch as he held a bag of frozen corn to the back of his head. Her foot bounced up and down on the beige carpet.

Dylan was simply amazing. No other word to describe him. He was her hero. If Alexis had opened the door...she shuddered, not wanting to think what might have happened She touched his shoulder. "Can I get you something, Dylan?"

"I'm fine, but you might want to calm down your friend."

Alexis seemed on the verge of a meltdown. After opening her patio door to allow in fresh air, she sat in an easy chair, but popped right back up and paced the room. Next, she walked out on the balcony, but now she sat in the chair once again, running fingers through her hair.

"I need a cigarette. Anyone here smoke?" Dylan asked.

"No you don't, Dylan." Reggie reached up and touched his arm. "I am not going to be the reason you start smoking again."

"Come on. One little cigarette wouldn't hurt."

"Yes, it—"

"Doesn't matter." Alexis broke in. "I don't

allow smoking in my apartment." She started pacing again.

"Yeah, all the smoke from one cigarette might wipe out the wonderful smell in here."

"I guess you're right, but I don't smoke, anyway." She looked at the police officer who sat at her dining room table filling out forms.

"Not me. Smoking's bad for your health."

"Yeah, like getting shot at isn't." Alexis flung herself into a chair. "I don't understand how they knew where to come."

"I found a bug in Reggie's apartment."

"A bug?" Reggie's face drained of color.

"A listening device." Dylan felt the bump on his head.

"I know what a bug is. I just can't believe there was one in my condo."

Alexis looked up from her chair. "Same here."

"Anyway, they heard our conversation about where you were going and then when you gave me your address, Alexis, you were giving it to them, too."

"We might as well have taken out a billboard announcing it to the world. Why would anyone want to kill me?" Reggie asked as she wiped at her eyes, not sure if the tears were from smoke, or the sheer terror of knowing someone wanted her dead. "I know people don't like lawyers, but this is taking the whole thing a bit too far. Don't you think?"

"I can't believe this, Reggie." Alexis picked up a throw pillow and hugged it.

"Well, believe it. I'm sure not going to fall apart and let them win." Her words were tough but her hands trembled, giving away the inner turmoil she fought. "If you hadn't come along right then..."

"I'm just glad I got here in time." He put his arm around her shoulder. Reggie leaned against him. As he gazed at her, she felt wrapped in a cocoon of his protection.

"So, now what, Officer?" Alexis bounced up once again. She stood in front of her patio door.

"The name is Ray, Ray Davis, Ms. Krinkle." He smiled at Alexis. "Or is it Mrs."

"Definitely, Miss. Call me Alexis."

Reggie's gaze followed as Alexis glanced down at the man's ring finger. Nothing. Alexis looked back up and Reggie swore she batted her eyelashes at the man. "You must need something to drink. I have sodas or water."

"Water would be just fine, Alexis."

Alexis walked towards the kitchen. Officer Ray followed behind her. "Let me help you."

After they left the room, Reggie leaned over to Dylan and whispered, "Did you see them flirting with each other. He's going to ask her out."

"What are you talking about?" Dylan looked baffled. "He's on duty."

"You just wait and see."

Alexis and the officer sauntered back in from the kitchen. Neither carried any water but Alexis's face was flushed and her eyes sparkled.

Officer Ray sported a grin. He looked at Reggie. "We'll keep investigating, but if I were you, I'd find a place to lay low for a while. We've got your cell phone number, and we'll be in touch."

Too exhausted to argue, Reggie thanked him.

Alexis walked with him to the door and the two had a whispered conference.

Reggie wanted to sink against Dylan, enjoy his warmth, his protectiveness and not have to think about her situation, but she didn't have such a luxury. She wouldn't jeopardize Alexis or Dylan again.

Alexis sauntered back towards Reggie and Dylan with a big smile.

"Did he ask you out for a date?"

"Yes, he did. I take advantage of the opportunities that come my way."

"Is that what you call this, Alexis?" Reggie snorted. "Someone terrorizes your whole condo building and you call it an opportunity to get a date."

"I believe in making lemonade out of a lemon. Nothing wrong with that." Alexis shrugged, her voice defensive.

"I'm just teasing. He's very cute." Reggie said.

"He is, isn't he? I asked Ray, and he said it would be safe for me to stay here as long as…you know…never mind. It doesn't matter."

"Don't worry, I'm leaving."

"I didn't mean…You can stay here." Alexis's face flushed red.

"I'm the one who should feel guilty. I put you in danger, but it won't happen again. I'll walk right out the front door so they see me leave. Then you'll be safe." Reggie jumped up with hands on her hips.

"But they—" Alexis looked distraught.

"If they want to shoot me, then I guess they

will. I'm getting sick of this." Reggie held up a hand.

Dylan took the bag of frozen corn off his head and set it on the coffee table. He touched Reggie's arm but she shook it off. "Whoa! Slow down, girl. No reason to throw out the baby with the bath water."

"What is that supposed to even mean?"

"It means calm dow—"

"I don't want to calm down." Even as she said the words, she sat back down.

"This whole thing is crazy. I just can't believe it." Alexis walked into the kitchen. This time she came back with three cans of pop and handed a diet to Reggie.

"We know there are at least two of them. It's beginning to feel like a conspiracy."

"It has to be about your work, Reggie." Dylan said as he opened his can. "I can't imagine what else it could be about."

"I mostly handle contracts." Reggie told him before taking a swig of the diet soda. The icy coldness soothed her raspy throat.

Dylan took a long slug of his soda. "Have there been any problems at work?"

"I've made a few mistakes but nothing to make someone want to kill me." She needed to get out of here. It wasn't safe for Alexis or Dylan. Reggie stood. "I'm leaving."

"You can't go. It's not safe." Alexis's lips quivered.

Reggie went to Alexis and hugged her. "Don't worry. I'll figure something out. I'm not stupid. I got through law school. I should be able to figure out what's going on, even if it kills me."

"Not funny, Reg." Alexis held Reggie tightly.

"I know. I have a warped sense of humor. So, shoot me. I'll call Sidney later to let her know what's going on."

Alexis looked at Dylan. "Are you going with her?"

"You betcha."

"You are not going with me. This is my problem, and I will figure it out on my own. I'm not putting anyone else in dan—"

"Not this time, Reggie." His words were soft as he walked towards her. His gaze locked on her and she was powerless to move. "I have no intention of abandoning you."

Reggie opened her mouth but no words came out. She wiped away more tears and finally choked out, "The smoke."

"The first thing we need to do is get you to my truck safely."

"Why not take my rental?" Reggie asked.

"No reason, except your things are in my truck and I thought you might want them."

"Including my laptop?"

He nodded.

"Great. I've got research to do if I'm going to get to the bottom of this."

Dylan arched an eyebrow at her. "Does this mean I get to come with you?"

Reggie bit her lip. She didn't want to endanger Dylan; it wouldn't be fair. "I can't ask you to put yourself in danger for me."

"I'm volunteering, and in fact, I'm not taking no for an answer. For the time being we're going to be as close as two peas in a pod." Dylan's eyes turned serious. "Reggie, trust me. I can keep you safe. I'm not going to let you down."

Everyone lets you down sooner or later. But she trusted him in a way she'd never trusted anyone before. She nodded.

"How many exits does this place have?" Dylan asked Alexis.

"Guests can only come in the front, but residents have key cards. Counting the garage and the front entrance…" She stopped and began counting on her fingers. "There's seven."

"Good. I can't believe they can have all of the doors covered. If they do, we're probably in more trouble than even I can handle."

"What makes you think you can handle it?" Reggie asked, more intrigued every moment by this handsome farmer. She'd thought of him as a cowboy, but now he appeared to be her knight in shining armor.

"Farmers have to know a little about a lot of different things. Who knows? I could come in handy."

"Are you going to just let her walk right out the front door?" Alexis asked.

"No way." Dylan looked at Alexis. "Got any ideas?"

Alexis looked thoughtful. "The safest thing would be the garage. You can drive up to the elevator door and she can jump right in."

"Sounds like a plan." Dylan nodded his agreement. "Do you have a ball cap or something to disguise me?"

"Sure hold on." Alexis went to her closet and

threw Dylan a ball cap. Then she held up a man's jacket. He arched an eyebrow.

"Don't ask."

"It's not much, but it could work." Dylan put on the makeshift disguise.

"Hand me your phone, and I'll put my cell number in it." Alexis held out a hand.

Dylan gave her his phone. She punched in some numbers and handed it back along with the key card to the underground garage. "Call us when you get inside the garage."

He looked at Reggie. Worry creased her brows. "Don't worry. I have more lives than a cat."

"Well, we've already used up two of them today."

****

Alexis walked with him to the door. She pulled him forward and gave him a peck on the cheek. "Thank you so much for helping Reggie. It's not easy for her to ask for help."

He picked a side entrance leading to the pool and tennis courts. At the door, he looked around. Nothing out of the ordinary, even the police and fire trucks were gone. Life in the big city had resumed.

From there, he hiked across the grass and climbed in his truck, breathing a sigh of relief. So far, so good. Now, he just had to get Reggie out of the area. Then, maybe she would be safe.

He stuck the key in the ignition, put his truck in gear, and slowly moved out, keeping his lights off. He scanned the area parking lot as he crept through it. Nothing suspicious. No people lingering. All the emergency vehicles gone. He pulled around to the garage entrance.

Still no cars following.

He slipped the access card in its slot and waited for the door to slide open. Too easy. The people who worked so hard to bug Reggie's apartment and set off smoke bombs wouldn't just let her get in a car and drive away. Unless they knew they could follow her.

The garage door opened and Dylan drove in.

Instead of calling Alexis, Dylan waited for the garage door to close. Someone who planted a bug in Reggie's apartment would be just as likely to attach a GPS. He climbed out and crawled under the truck. It took only seconds to see the device right where he would have hidden it.

Only it wasn't a GPS tracking device.

His trained military gaze immediately recognized it.

A bomb.

14

The phone in Dylan's pocket rang. He jerked and bumped his head on the truck's manifold. He slid from under the vehicle and rubbed his head as he flipped open the phone. "What?" He sat up.

"Are you in the garage? What's wrong? What's taking you so long?" Alexis's voice was filled with worry.

"We have a situation. Don't come"—The elevator door slid open—"out."

Reggie bolted out of the elevator with Alexis close behind.

"I said not to come out." He flipped the phone shut. "This is not some silly fire drill in elementary school. Instead of getting detention for not following the rules, you could get dead."

"What's the problem?" Reggie propelled herself towards him and the truck.

He unfolded his long legs and stood. He held up a hand as if he was a crossing guard. "Please, don't come any closer."

Alexis nodded towards Reggie. "I tried to stop her, but she wouldn't listen."

Reggie stopped, but folded her arms, glaring at Alexis, then at Dylan. "I wasn't waiting one second longer in that steel tomb. What could be so bad?"

"There's a bomb under my truck. Now, both of you get back in the elevator."

Eyes wide, Alexis retraced her steps backward towards the elevator while Reggie moved forward. "Are you sure it's a bomb?"

"I was a bomb specialist in the Marines, among other things."

"You were a what?" Reggie's voice registered shock.

"Just get back." Dylan pointed at the elevator. "If it blows you'll be safe from the blast in the elevator.." Dylan stretched out next to the truck to get a closer look. Underneath the belly and near the tailpipe nestled a black metal box with eight wires. Four on each side curved up and out like spider legs. A beautiful, but deadly black widow spider, complete with a flashing red hourglass, awaiting its prey.

Warm air tickled his cheek and neck. He turned towards the warmth and found himself inches away from two enticing green eyes. He inhaled an arousing scent of lilac, feeling the heat of passion between them.

"What...do you see?" Her eyes traveled to his mouth. She licked her lips and took a deep breath.

He needed to concentrate. The bomb. He had to diffuse the bomb.

He jumped up, taking her with him. She trembled against his chest. Or was he the one trembling? His breath was heavy, a fire raging out of control. He wanted to press his lips against hers.

Her face dropped out of sight. She was down and peering under the truck.

Like a giant fishhook, his arm circled her waist, pulling her up, and setting her on her feet.

"I want to see it." Reggie wobbled.

"Did you ever hear 'curiosity *killed* the cat?'" He gently touched her shoulders to steady her.

"I'm not a cat."

"My point exactly. You *don't* have nine lives to play around with. Please go back into the elevator and let me take a look." He went to the back of the truck and opened a tool box. He grabbed a flashlight and wire cutters.

"Maybe, we…we…should just call the cops?" Alexis said, rising up behind a Chevy Tahoe parked next to the elevator.

"The killer is probably outside waiting for us to leave, so he can make sure Reggie is inside before he detonates the bomb. If he sees the cops he may detonate it early, before I have a chance to diffuse it."

"Are you nuts?" Alexis squeaked. "You can't."

"Sure I can." He smiled and tried to look reassuring for the ladies. "It's not my first rodeo with a bomb."

"Alexis is right, Dylan. We should call the cops and let them handle this." Reggie grabbed hold of his arm in an attempt to pull him towards the elevator.

He shook his head. "If the bad guys see police descending on us, we risk them detonating the bomb. A lot of people could get hurt."

He watched Reggie's demeanor change from scared to business-like. She stood straighter. It was as if she mentally accepted his decision and her responsibility. Admiration bloomed in his heart and mind.

"What can I do to help?" She asked, her voice firm.

"Wait with Alexis by the elevator...just in case."

"I'm not going anywhere." Reggie gave Dylan a hard stare.

"Do you have a death wish?" he asked between clenched teeth. Why wouldn't she just let him keep her safe?

"Do you?" she yelled at him.

"Reggie, you need to listen to him." Alexis called from inside the elevator.

Reggie turned and glared at her friend.

Alexis threw up her hands. "Fine, be a hero...but this Chicken Little is going to wait right here just in case the sky falls."

The elevator door slid shut.

****

Reggie breathed a sigh of relief. No reason for Alexis to be hurt, but she refused to shirk her responsibility. She was the reason there was a bomb under Dylan's truck. If Dylan insisted on doing this, she would be there to help.

Dylan lay down on the dirty concrete and crawled back under the truck. She stared at the floor, wondering how many bugs and spiders were crawling around. Taking a deep breath, she did the same. She scooted close to him.

"Reggie, please go to the elevator with Alexis." His finger trailed down her cheek. "I don't want anything to happen to you."

She scooted closer. The heat of his body soothed her frayed nerves. "And I don't want anything to happen to you. If you think you can do this, then I trust you."

"Make yourself useful. Hold this." He handed her the flashlight.

Without a word, she took the flashlight. Her heart raced and sweat oozed from her palms, but she didn't dare move the light. Dylan needed it.

God...I'm not good at this praying thing. Please help us. Help Dylan. I don't want him to die for me. Please keep him safe...

"What are you doing?"

"Why are you whispering? The bomb can't hear you. I'm going to disarm it," he said in his normal voice.

"Do you know how?" Incredulity colored her voice.

"I know you think I'm just a country hick, but I've done this a million times."

"Really?"

"No, but I have done it a few times." He took her hand and guided it. "Flash the light right there."

She did as she was told. The light bobbed up and down from her shaking hand.

"Use both your hands, Reggie."

She steadied the light and he moved the wire cutters towards the wires. Reggie noticed his hands shook as well. He separated the wires and snipped one of them. Nothing happened.

"It's over." He told her. He snipped more wires and slid the device off the muffler.

"What are you going to do with it?"

He looked around. He walked over to a trash can and put the device in it. "I'll call the police and they can take care of it."

"Are you sure it's safe?"

"For the moment. Tell Alexis goodbye. We need to leave." He handed her his cell.

The elevator door slid open and Alexis rushed back into the garage. The two friends hugged, Then Reggie climbed in the truck.

"You've got my cell phone number. If the police need to talk with me, give it to them."

Reggie slid close to Dylan. She searched his face for fear, but a confident cowboy looked back.

"Ready?" he asked her.

For a moment, she thought of jumping out and running away. What if he was injured or even killed because of her? Could she live with that? She didn't know how she'd ended up with this amazing man. She'd probably be dead right now if not for him. Blowing out stale air and her fear, she nodded.

They pulled out of the dimly lit garage into the darkness. Streetlights glared. It took a moment for her eyes to adjust. Her gaze jumped around the outside parking lot. She expected more gunfire or explosions, or some equally horrifying event, after the incident in the garage.

"There they are." Dylan announced in a voice as calm as if he'd just ordered a hamburger through the drive-thru. How could he stay so calm? "In the black SUV over to your right by the second elm tree."

"What makes you think so? I can't see anything."

"Exactly. The windows are so dark you can't see them. As we drive past get the plate number. We'll call it into the police."

"Maybe, we shouldn't drive past them."

He reached over and patted her hand. "It's OK, they aren't going to do anything to us. They've got their ace in the hole, or so they think."

Dylan and Reggie drove past the car. She squinted. "The plates have mud on them. I can't see the numbers."

"Very professional."

At the stop sign, he glanced at Reggie. "Fasten your seatbelt. We've got to get out of here before they realize we aren't going to explode."

"You told me you were a farmer. You didn't mention being a bomb expert, as well."

"I didn't know I'd be needing that skill any longer. Put on your seatbelt."

She grinned. "You really are the seatbelt police."

"And don't forget it."

She reached for her seatbelt. Dylan turned onto the road and then hit the gas. They surged forward with unexpected speed. Reggie turned around to watch the car. "They're following us."

"Tell me where to go. Cleveland's your town, not mine."

"Turn left on Chester. There's an exit to the highway a few blocks away."

His gaze flitted from one side of the road to the other, and then he ran through the red light. Shocked, she stared at him, then turned to the back window to watch the black SUV. "I see them."

"Which way? East or West?"

She had no idea what to tell him, but finally said, "East."

Instead of going east, he took the ramp marked west. Why had he asked if he wasn't going to listen? As they sped down the ramp, she glanced at the speedometer, it showed seventy-three. She hoped traffic wouldn't be too heavy, because it didn't look as if he planned on stopping. He merged into the traffic without a problem.

"You went the wrong way."

"I know. We don't actually want them to know which way we're going. Since they're following us, they'll see us going west-bound. When I lose them, they'll keep heading west. I hope."

Reggie felt dumb for even bringing it up. "Makes sense."

"Can you see them?"

She twisted in her seat and stared at the traffic behind them. "I see a black SUV, but I don't know if it's them."

Dylan switched lanes and hit the gas. The cars blurred as they passed. Reggie was amazed when the ever-cautious Dylan reached eighty-five miles-per-hour. After passing several exits, he changed lanes and at the last moment exited the highway.

"Can you get me to another exit?"

Within moments they were back on the highway going east. Reggie looked around. No sign of the black SUV.

Reggie let out her breath. "Did we lose them?"

"We'll see. Keep an eye out to be sure."

Neither of them spoke for the next several miles. Reggie's mind swirled from the day's events. Had it been just hours ago when they'd walked up to her condo with the only goal being to clean it up? Now her only goal was to stay alive.

A part of her wanted to curl up in a fetal position and cry, but the healthier part kept telling her she'd been through tough times before and survived. She would survive this, as well. Efforts to think of a worse experience failed.

There was the time a foster father had been so angry at her for sassing him he'd put her in a closet for two days, but it hadn't been as bad as it could have been. The foster mother had given her food and insulin when he wasn't looking, and given her a pot to use for a toilet.

"What are you doing?"

She jumped. She'd been locked in a closet. Taking a deep breath, she wished she were in that closet at the moment. "I was trying to think of a worse experience than this one."

"Why?" He turned slightly towards her.

"When I'm going through a bad experience, I think about all the bad things I've been through. Then, I tell myself I've been through worse, and I will survive this, too."

"Sounds depressing."

"Problem is I'm having trouble thinking of something worse than this." She bit her lip for a moment. "What do you do?"

"I pray."

"Really? A big strong Marine like you?" It wasn't the answer she expected. She thought back to her own prayer only minutes earlier. The first time she'd prayed in years. Why would God even listen to her?

"Yep."

"I used to pray when I was young, but nothing ever changed, so I gave up on God."

"That's OK but God hasn't given up on you." He gave her a slow smile.

"How can you say that? Someone is trying to kill me and I don't have the vaguest idea why. It doesn't sound like God's on my side." The anger in her voice surprised her.

"Yeah, but he arranged for us to meet. And you might not know it, but meeting me was a good thing. Together with God's help, we're going to get to the bottom of this."

"You don't really believe all that stuff, do you?"

"Every bit of it. God's kept me safe through many things, and he kept you safe today."

"Have you ever been chased before by bad guys trying to kill a woman you barely know?"

"Can't say that I have, until now."

15

In little more than an hour, a billboard welcomed Reggie and Dylan to Pennsylvania. Reggie shuddered. She'd grown up in the state, but had no desire to come back. When Dylan asked what direction, she hadn't expected him to drive all this way

"I've been thinking," Dylan announced.

"Not me. I've been daydreaming about a trip to a south sea island. Short of that, I'm not sure how to get out of this mess."

"At least you haven't lost your sense of humor." He laughed. "First things, first. We'll find a motel with WiFi. After you rest, you can check your work files to see if something jumps out at you."

"Sounds like a plan."

When the turnpike ended, they were assaulted with motels on every side. They picked one that advertised wireless Internet, and then pulled up to the lobby to register. Dylan opened his door and stretched his back. Reggie did the same.

"What are you doing?" He asked.

"I don't want to stay here by myself."

"Nobody's following us." Dylan assured her.

"You can't be sure of that." She looked around. Paranoia was getting the best of her.

"I'm pretty sure." Dylan looked steady and reassuring.

"OK, thank you." She went towards the lobby door without another word, recalling his military experience and finding comfort in that thought.

****

Dylan walked into his motel room carrying Reggie's luggage still stuck in the garbage bags.

He sat on the bed and willed his adrenaline to slow down. He searched his pockets for a stick of gum and found one. He stared at it for a moment. What he really wanted was a cigarette, but the gum would have to do for now.

God, thank you for keeping us safe today. I know you brought Reggie to me so I could help her and I'm going to do my best. I ask for your protection and your wisdom to do that. In Jesus's name I pray, Amen.

He picked up the trash bags and walked over to the door separating their rooms. He knocked. No response. He waited for a moment before rapping once more. Still nothing. He opened it.

****

Reggie sat on the bed staring at a blank wall.

"Are you all right?"

His voice gave her a sense of comfort.

"Yes. No. I don't know." She gave him a half-hearted grin. "I think I'm in shock."

"Pretty normal response under the circumstances." He laid the garbage bags on the bed. "Here're your things."

She stared at the bags, then up at him, surprise etched in her face. "You brought me garbage?"

"I was trying to camouflage the fact you were hiding out somewhere other than your apartment. Not that it mattered. Thanks to the bug I found in your apartment, they knew exactly where you were going."

"What next? Guns. Bombs. Car chases. Bugs." Her lips trembled as she tried to smile. "It's like a movie. And a bad movie at that."

"Oh, I don't know. I think the leading lady is quite fetching, if you ask me." He walked over and sat down on the bed beside her. "I know you're scared, but God's watching over us. It's going to be OK."

She shook her head and wiped away a tear. "It doesn't feel like it will ever be OK again."

"We're going to figure this thing out together, you'll see." He stood. "I'm going out to buy some more ammo."

Startled, she jumped off the bed. "Why would you need that?"

"To put in my gun."

"You crossed a state line with a gun?" Her voice turned shrill. "That must be against the law."

"Actually, it's not in Pennsylvania, but I can..."

"It's not? It should be. That's what's wrong with—"

"That's a matter of opinion. In case you've forgotten, someone is after you. Guns will help me protect you."

"I hate guns." She shook her head and

shuddered.

"Do you want to have a debate about the right to bear arms or do you want to be safe?"

She stared at him for several long moments. Her world shifted as she thought about the answer to his question. Taking a deep breath, she sat back down. "I want to be safe."

"That's what I thought." He walked over and touched her shoulder. "Maybe you should take a bath or a nap or something while I'm gone."

"Gone?" She shook her head. "You can't leave me here alone. What if they find me?"

"That's not going to happen. We lost them back in Cleveland. There's no way they can find us."

"So far today, they've used guns, bugs and bombs. Are you sure?"

"I thought you might want to rest while I run some errands and get you some food. It has to be time for you to eat."

"I've been nibbling on the crackers. But I do need more food. Let me check my blood sugar."

She rummaged through her purse until she found what she needed. A quick check showed her glucose was a little low. She swayed ever so slightly.

Dylan moved towards her.

"I'm exhausted, but..." She was so tired. She looked at the bed and back to Dylan. She felt incapable of making a decision, even one as simple as to stay or go. "I need, I need..."

He put his arms around her.

Even as she tried to push him away, the tears began.

He held her while she sobbed. When the tears slowed, he took her chin in his hand and lifted her face up. "I promise I'm going to do everything I can to keep you safe. I'm not going to leave you."

He slowly leaned down and their lips met. Sweet and gentle, the kiss lasted but a moment, but she savored it.

"You lay down and take a nap. I'll have a pizza delivered. After that we can run the errands together."

"Really?"

"Really."

Dylan smiled at her. Her heart skipped a beat but her mind told her to stop being ridiculous. It was the situation, not the man. She had nothing in common with a gun-toting farmer who'd risked his life to help a stranger.

16

Shadows jumped around the darkened motel room as Reggie's eyes adjusted to the dimness. She felt better, but scenes from the day crowded back into her consciousness. Trent at her apartment, being shot at, the fire alarm, the bomb.

A bomb. Hard to imagine. It had to be a humongous blunder. Nobody wanted to kill her—a junior attorney and an orphan. Obviously, a case of mistaken identity. But she had to fix it before she could return to her life.

She'd never complain again about all the tedious paperwork or feeling like a lackey for the senior partners. She wanted to be bored again.

Hopefully, the police had caught the perpetrators already. She would call Alexis to see if she knew anything. Officer Ray was, no doubt, keeping her informed. Reggie smiled. Only Alexis would end up with a potential date after what happened.

Dylan. Her finger touched the spot where he'd kissed her. What a surprise Dylan turned out to be. A simple farmer…a former Marine. She sat up and sniffed. Pizza. Her stomach rumbled and her mouth watered. Her nose led the way.

****

Dylan looked up when Reggie walked in. She was a beautiful woman even with tousled hair and puffy eyes.

He had to stop thinking like that. Reggie was in serious trouble, God had put her in his path for a reason—and it wasn't to seduce her when she was vulnerable. *Keep your mind on the job at hand.*

He waved at her. "Hey, sleepyhead."

"How long did I sleep?" Reggie attempted to smooth down her hair.

"Not long. Not even an hour." He gestured at the bed. "We've got vittles. I ordered pizza, but the take-out place had Chinese, too. So, I thought some Chinese vegetables and rice would be good and I had them throw in some egg rolls, too."

"Are you sure you got enough? Did you already eat?"

"No, it just got here a few minutes ago. The smell's probably what woke you. The motel owners assure me, it's the best place around." He handed her a plastic plate and grabbed one for himself. He scooped food and she did the same. She picked a diet soda and set it on the nightstand.

"You must have a great metabolism. The way you eat. Do you work out?"

"Yeah, I do. It's called farming. I call it God's workout. It keeps you fit and healthy and pays the bills at the same time. Can't ask for more than that."

"I guess that's better than paying for a gym membership you never use." She tore open a packet of hot mustard, squirted it onto her plate, then dipped her egg roll and took a bite. Her eyes watered. "Mmm. That's good. Just the way I like it."

"Liar."

"Am not. Did you get some rest, too?"

Dylan ate his eggroll in two bites. "Not really. I called my mom and told her I'd be gone for a few days. She and dad will take care of the farm while I'm away."

"Oh, Dylan, I'm sorry I got you involved in this. You have your own life to take care of. You don't ne—"

He gently placed his hand on her chin and lifted her face. Their gazes met. "This is exactly where I want to be. Stop worrying about me."

Reggie nodded. "Did you tell her…what happened?"

He shook his head as he shoveled half the slice of pizza in his mouth. "No reason to make her worry."

"I guess I should call Alexis and let her know we're OK." Reggie took a sip of her diet pop.

"Already did, but you can call her if you want. She's at the office with your boss. They're going through the files trying to figure out if this has anything to do with your work."

She blinked several times. "Wow. You've been busy. It almost makes me feel guilty for sleeping like a baby in there."

"It shouldn't. You needed to rest."

"I couldn't think but I'm better now. Did you tell them where we were?" She pulled a slice of pepperoni off the pizza and popped it in her mouth.

"I thought it was better to keep the

information to myself. We can keep in touch by cell phone." He shook his head

"What happened with the bomb?"

"Cleveland called in the FBI and they're checking for fingerprints or any other forensic evidence. So far, nothing. They found a bomb on your rental, too."

"I can't believe what's happened to me today." She stood, threw her plate in the trashcan and took another sip of her drink.

"Did you eat enough?"

"Yes." Reggie changed the subject. "How did you get to be a farmer?"

He shrugged. "By default, I guess you could say. My dad's a farmer, His dad was a farmer and so on. My brother had no interest in farming, so that meant me."

"I didn't know you had a brother."

"He lives in Chicago. When my dad had a heart attack and needed some help, I cut my time in the Marines short and here I am."

"The Marines let you do that?"

"Hardship. This country needs its farmers. I had planned to make the Marines my career but I've grown to love farming." It hadn't been his first choice at the time, but God's plan was the right one.

"But it sounds so hard, so unreliable. Look at what happened to those people you know who are losing their farm."

"The Starks. They're good people, but they didn't manage their farm the way it should have been. I'm not blaming them, but they made a few mistakes."

"But I thought it was the drought." She picked up the eggroll, but set it back down without taking a bite.

"The drought was just the straw that broke the camel's back."

"So, your farm's not in trouble?"

"Not at the moment, but farming isn't for the faint of heart. There are government regulations, the weather, low prices, and anything else you can think of."

"Doesn't sound like an easy life."

"It's not, but I love it."

"How long have you been farming?"

"Is that a sneaky way to find out how old I am?" He winked at her.

Reggie's face turned pink and she tilted her head and smiled. "Maybe."

She tugged at his heart. She acted tough, but vulnerability was well hidden. "About four years. Enough about me. My life's boring. Tell me about yours."

"Well, my life is anything *but* boring." Laughing felt good. "What a mess, will we ever figure it all out?" Reggie pointed at her laptop sitting on the small round table beside the bed. "What were you checking on the computer?"

"Just catching up on email and business things. Farmers are hi-tech nowadays, you know." He drew out the words in a ridiculous hillbilly drawl.

Reggie stuck out her tongue as she cleaned up their mess. Her eyes landed on a pack of cigarettes. She picked them up. "What's this?"

"I know. I know. I ordered them in a moment

of weakness but I didn't open them. Yet."

"Good thing. I don't want to be responsible for you starting again. Of course, smoking's probably better for your health than I am."

"You may be right."

"What should I do with them?"

"Throw 'em out."

"Good choice. What now? It's probably too late to go to a gun shop or where ever you go to buy bullets."

"It's never too late for one of the super stores."

"Which one?"

He named one, "You've heard of the place, haven't you?"

"Of course." She rolled her eyes. "After that, what then?"

"Then, we're going to come back here and get a good night's rest. One thing's for sure, we can't figure much out if our brains are so tired they won't work."

17

Dylan drove back to the hotel. Along with ammo, he'd bought two pairs of jeans, T-shirts and assorted other supplies they might need, including snacks.

As he turned the corner, his heart took a nosedive. Lights flashed on three different police cruisers and people milled about in the motel parking lot. Their problems had found them once again. He glanced at Reggie.

"We've got trouble." He pointed to the parking lot.

"You don't think that has something to do with us, do you?" Her voice sounded panicked.

"It might not, but I don't think we should go back there until we know."

"Why not call the motel?" Reggie pulled her cell phone from her purse.

"Couldn't hurt." Dylan agreed.

She punched in the number for directory assistance, then allowed it to connect to the motel. "We were about to pull in, but noticed all the police cars. Is there a problem?" After a moment, she asked, "What kind of a break-in?" She rolled her eyes at Dylan as she listened. "I'm registered there and I want to know if it's safe to come back to my room."

Dylan smiled.

Her voice changed from sweet to firmly in control as she went in to attorney mode. "I don't care about your rules. I was under the impression your establishment was safe but I can see I was misinformed. I want to know what rooms were broken into and I want to know now. Or—" She hesitated then asked another question. "And have these criminals been apprehended?"

A moment later, she thanked the clerk and hung up. She bit her lips and take a deep breath. "It was our rooms and they didn't catch the thieves."

Dylan couldn't believe it. He'd been sure they'd be OK after they lost the SUV. He'd underestimated them. "I'm sorry. I guess we shouldn't have registered under our own names or used our credit cards."

The color drained from her face. Reggie stared ahead, not moving, not talking. Finally, she turned towards him, her gaze seemed to beg him to make it all go away. "My things are back there."

He'd failed her. "Sweetheart, but if we go back they might be watching for us. We'd be sitting ducks."

"You're right. They're just things. But what do we do now?" She visibly straightened, her words strong.

He was proud of her. "Now, we get smart. We're going to an ATM and we'll withdraw our limit so we have cash. From here on out, cash only. No more electronic trails to follow."

"Then what?"

"No more cell phones. We have to assume

they can access those records as well. "

"I just don't know what to do. I'm just…" She stared out the truck window. "What about later?"

"You don't need to do anything, Reggie. God put the two of us together for a reason. I'm going to keep you safe and find out what's going on."

"How can you do that? You're a farmer."

Looking her way, he winked. "Yeah, but I'm a really good farmer."

****

Dylan's singing drifted down to her subconscious. As Reggie struggled to wake up, the events of yesterday crashed back like a tsunami.

Her neck and back hurt from sleeping lopsided in the truck. She opened her eyes and stretched. The sky was beginning to lighten as the morning made its way over the horizon.

"What are you singing?"

"That, darling, is one of the best songs of the twentieth century."

"Hmph, must have been before my time." She looked over at Dylan.

Dark circles under his eyes told her Dylan was exhausted, but still he smiled and sang. Didn't the guy ever get in a bad mood? "Where are we?"

"Technically, we're in Maryland, but we're about to cross over to Berkeley Springs, West Virginia."

After the fiasco at the motel, he'd encouraged her to go to sleep so he could think. She'd been happy to comply.

"Why?"

"I have a buddy who can help us."

"Another farmer?"

Undaunted by her skepticism, Dylan grinned. "No, another ex- Marine who's a computer nerd. He's a genius."

"I didn't know Marines could be computer nerds." She reached in the bag at her feet. "I have to eat something. Want an apple?"

"Sure."

She pulled out a Golden Delicious and a Red Delicious. She held them up. "You pick."

"I like 'em both." She handed the red apple to Dylan. Both munched on the fruit.

"Does he know we're coming?"

"No cell phones, remember? But it won't be a problem."

She couldn't imagine the man would be happy with them showing up without warning, but who was she to argue. "Because he's a Marine, right?"

"No, because he's my friend."

"It must be nice to have friends like that." Making friends had never been easy for her. She had plenty of acquaintances but...that didn't mean they were friends.

"Alexis seems like a good friend."

"She is." Reggie shrugged. "I trust Alexis, but I'm not so sure about any of the others." Her first instinct was to tell him she didn't need anyone, but the argument died in her throat. She wouldn't be alive if Dylan hadn't chosen to help her.

He checked the rearview mirror. "You need to pick better friends."

Reggie smiled at him. "I already have."

"You can count on me Reggie. We will get to the bottom of this." He put the apple core into the ashtray and placed his hand over hers.

The warmth made her feel safe, and for a moment she couldn't breathe. "I haven't even said thank you for all you're doing for me. I don't know how I'm ever going to repay you."

"I haven't gotten you out of this mess, yet. So, don't thank me now. And as for repaying me, I'll think of a way," he said with a wink.

Her feelings for Dylan were burrowing in her heart like the roots of a live oak. Was he falling for her, too? Maybe he just wanted light hearted companionship. She decided to play it casual.

"Why, Dylan. I thought you Christians didn't think about things like sex."

"Oh, we think about things—plenty. We're human after all, but I want to find the right person to share my love with. Not that we aren't tempted, we just try to make the right choices when situations come up."

He'd been a perfect gentleman and paid for two motel rooms. He was acting honorable. The wonder of it washed over her. A man who had strong convictions about treating women with respect and considering her feelings. His next question reaffirmed her thoughts.

"How are you feeling? Do you need a new glucose meter, or whatever you call that thing?"

"I can get along without it. Thanks to my store's national pharmacy system, I have insulin and syringes. That's the important stuff. I don't have to measure blood sugar. It's easier with it, but I'll be fine as long as I keep eating right."

"Good. Is there anything I need to know or do?"

"Not a thing." *Just keep us safe.*

18

Twenty minutes after leaving the gas station, Reggie gripped the door handle and stared at tree tops in the valley below. After crossing the Potomac River into West Virginia, they'd driven through Berkeley Springs and then up this mountain. Curve after curve, they'd climbed higher and higher.

"What kind of place are you taking me to?"

"It's a bit remote. Billy Clyde doesn't like to be around people. He's a loner."

"You don't say. Do you actually know where you're going?"

"Sure, I've been here a few times. This is the main road."

"The main road." She looked over the edge and tightened her grip. "Do any of your other friends live in a normal place on a normal road?"

"I am sure the people of Paw Paw would think this is a normal road."

"Sorry." She muttered and dug her nails deeper into the armrest.

"No problem. This is Cacapon Mountain. It's an amazing sight. Look over there."

Instead of gazing at the trees, she closed her eyes. Her foot pressed into the floor, but without a brake; it didn't help. Hearing a click of his turn signal, she opened an eye to find them pulling off the road. The truck slowed to a stop.

"You can breathe now. We've stopped for a moment. Look at that." Dylan pointed at the valley below them.

Reggie looked. It was truly magnificent. Browns, oranges, reds, and golds blended into a beautiful montage of color below them. The sun peeked over the trees coloring the sky in pinkish purple and blue.

"There's a verse in the Bible that says God clearly shows His power by the things He has made. We aren't just looking at some pretty trees. We're looking at God's power."

The wonder in his tone caused her to glance at him. His face was serene as he gazed out at the multitude of fall colors. How could he look so calm when her stomach was churning from stress? He turned and saw she was watching him and not the view.

"What? Do you want to ask me something?"

"How can you be so calm when you're sitting beside someone who is being stalked to be killed?"

"That's easy. I trust God. He'll take care of us one way or the other."

"Meaning?"

"He'll either keep me safe, or take me home." He shrugged. "Either way, it's a win-win situation."

It sounded so simple when Dylan said it, but where had God been all those nights she'd cried herself to sleep, alone and afraid? Reggie shook her head. "I just don't understand you or your faith. If God is real, why do so many bad things happen?"

"Another easy one. You need to come up with some harder questions, Reggie. God doesn't do evil, people do. When He created us, He gave us free will. We make our choices. Unfortunately, a lot of the bad choices of other people affect all of us."

"You make it sound so simple."

"Reggie. Look out there. You can't tell me you can't see God's magnificence." He touched her shoulder.

She scanned the valley below them. "I suppose not." She spoke quietly but her next words were tinged with bitterness. "But what's God ever done for me?"

"Aside from the fact He sent His Son down here so you could spend forever with Him in heaven, He also sent me to you." He grinned. "Think about it. You needed someone who would know to look for hidden microphone bugs and who knew how to defuse a bomb. There are no coincidences in God's plan, Reggie. You were blessed the day you crashed into me."

"I don't think so. We both know you're the one—" She gave him a mock punch on his arm.

"That's not the way the officer saw it." He said, and then laughed. He snapped his seatbelt back in place and waited. After she'd done the same, he pulled back on the road.

They descended slowly down the mountain. He offered her a stick of gum, but she refused. He shrugged, unwrapped it, and popped it in his own mouth.

"Great. Now, we're going back down the

mountain."

"That's the way it usually works." He started singing. "What goes up must—"

"Very funny." She laughed. "I can't believe you actually know a song that wasn't written in Nashville. You stop singing and keep your eyes on the road, Mister."

"Yes, ma'am."

A town was nestled in the side of the mountain. A sign welcomed them to Great Cacapon, population 1379. Not much of a town, a gas station, a school and a small restaurant were the highlights. They passed through it.

When they arrived at the bottom of the mountain, Reggie unclenched her fingers from around the door handle. A large red, white, and blue sign welcomed her to Paw Paw, West Virginia. The town appeared even smaller than Great Cacapon.

"You must feel right at home here." She teased with a smile.

"Is that a wisecrack about my hometown?"

"Yes, it is."

"Not very nice. That's all I've got to say. Not very nice."

Amazed at herself, she laughed. Someone was trying to kill her and yet, she felt safe and almost lighthearted, as if the two of them were just on a weekend trip.

If Dylan and his family were examples of what happened when God was a part of one's life, she might just need to spend some time examining her own relationship with God…if she lived through this ordeal.

Dylan laid his hand on hers. It felt right. She tried to tell herself it was ridiculous. She wasn't cut out to be a farmer's wife. Just the idea made her smile.

"A penny for your thoughts."

Her face grew warm. No way did she want him to know what she was thinking. "I'm thinking it's time for another apple and some cheese."

His raised eyebrow told her he didn't believe she'd been thinking about food. "If you want, but we'll be at Billy Clyde's in a minute. He might be persuaded to fix a real breakfast for us."

As he said the words, he turned off on a dirt road in the middle of trees. After a hundred yards, the dirt road turned to nothing more than a grass path. They bumped along the path at a snail's pace. "I guess you made a wrong turn."

"Oh, ye, of little faith."

She looked around. All she saw were trees and bushes. Certainly, nobody lived there unless they lived in a tree house. "Just admit it, Dylan. You made a wrong turn."

"City girl." He grinned. "Stick with me, you'll see all kinds of country things."

A part of her said no way, but the other part melted at his words, until the lawyer in her took over. *Stop being a silly romantic. You've got real problems. Someone wants you dead. This is not the time, nor the place, to be acting like a love-struck teenager.*

They came to an abrupt stop. Bushes blocked their way. She smirked at Dylan. "I told—"

Dylan held up a hand and jumped out of his truck. He walked to the bushes. She gaped as he pushed his way through, revealing a hidden gate and fencing. Dylan hit a button on a silver box sitting atop the fence gate. It felt as if she were in a James Bond movie. She rolled down her window to listen.

"Billy Clyde. It's Dylan Monroe."

"So, I see." A voice came through the box. "Who's the beautiful woman? Don't tell me you went and found someone who would marry your ugly self?"

How did he see her? Must be a camera somewhere. She looked around, but couldn't find it. What person hid his house behind bushes and trees, and had surveillance cameras? Someone who had something to hide. Worry seeped in for a moment, but then she relaxed. Dylan wouldn't bring her some place dangerous.

"I'll explain after you let us in."

"Sure, come on in, buddy. Park your truck in the open bay."

As Dylan walked back to the truck the gate slid open, with the bushes still attached. When Dylan got in the truck, Reggie looked at him. "Are those bushes real?"

"They are. Didn't I tell you that Billy Clyde is a genius? And as with all geniuses, they have a variety of talents and interests. He's not just a computer nerd. You'll like him."

They bumped along for several hundred more yards before it opened up to a green grassy area. She'd expected to see a shanty of some sort, since Billy Clyde lived out in the middle of nowhere. Instead, a huge log cabin sat in the middle of the hidden oasis.

She only hoped it had running water and indoor plumbing.

Attached to the log cabin was a long garage. One of the garage doors stood open waiting for them. They pulled in and the door immediately closed. At least, the place had electricity.

19

Before Reggie could open the truck door, a man walked out of the house. Billy Clyde looked like a Marine. He stood way over six feet and could pass for a body builder.

African-American. She hadn't expected that. With a name like Billy Clyde and living in the mountains of West Virginia, she'd assumed he'd be a redneck of some sort. A geeky, skinny computer whiz, pale, with black glasses taped in the middle and a pocket protector.

Don't be so judgmental.

The man wore his hair military style, but it was sprinkled with enough gray to make him appear distinguished, wise, and a decade or more older than Dylan.

"Monroe. What are you doing here, boy?" The man's booming voice filled the garage.

"We've got a little problem." Dylan stepped out of the truck and walked over. The two men clasped each other by the shoulder.

Reggie hopped out and walked up to them.

"That explains why a beautiful woman is with you. I knew there had to be a logical reason. For a minute, I thought maybe you kidnapped her." The giant of a man turned to Reggie and held out his hand. "Glad to meet you. My name's Billy Clyde

Addams but you can just call me Billy."

Billy's hand dwarfed her own as they shook. "I'm Reggie Meyers. Sorry we just dropped in like this but—"

"It's not a problem. Have you eaten breakfast yet?"

"No, but we don't want to be any trouble." Reggie answered.

Dylan started laughing. "Don't let her kid you, Billy Clyde. She was just telling me she was starving and hoped you had food."

Her face grew warm as she glared at Dylan. Didn't he have any manners? "I never said—"

"Good, I was just about to fix something for myself, anyway. Welcome to my humble abode, Reggie."

He opened the door and motioned for her to go in, but Dylan put a hand on her arm.

"Where are the dogs, Billy Clyde?"

"Don't worry, they're outside." Billy shook his head and chuckled. Looking at her, he said, "He's afraid of my cute little puppies."

"I wouldn't exactly call those German Shepherds of yours puppies or little." Dylan removed his hand.

Reggie was expecting to see an old-fashioned cook stove or even a fireplace. Instead, she stepped into a modern spacious kitchen. She smiled to hide her embarrassment.

"What, did you think I was living in some log cabin out in the middle of nowhere like a hermit?" Billy Clyde laughed. "Not me. I like my luxuries."

"I can see that. I admit I expected things to be a little more primitive, but your home is beautiful."

"I'll show you around later. Any requests for breakfast?" He looked at Reggie.

"Maybe an egg, and if you have some high fiber bread, I'll take that."

"Reggie's diabetic. She needs to eat healthy and unfortunately, we haven't had much time for eating since we found the bomb under my truck." Dylan explained.

"Dylan, my boy, you draw danger like a magnet." Billy nodded for them to be seated. "Take a load off. I'll cook breakfast while you give me every detail, and don't leave anything out."

Reggie stared open-mouthed.

Dylan had just told him a bomb had been under his truck and he acted as if they had a flat tire. Who was this man?

Billy motioned them towards the breakfast island in the middle of the huge room.

Reggie and Dylan sat next to each other on stools facing Billy.

"That's the problem. We have no idea what's going on, except someone wants Reggie dead."

She thought Billy would be shocked by Dylan's announcement, but he nodded and kept cooking. Dylan and Reggie took turns telling him what had happened the day before. The whole thing sounded like a Hollywood film. She couldn't believe it had happened in one day and to her.

Billy brought over platters filled with toast, scrambled eggs, sausage and bacon, and set a bowl in front of Reggie.

"Grits. They're low on the Glycemic Index. Very healthy or so my nutritionist tells me. The bread is multi-grain, as well. My nutritionist is a bully.." He patted his belly, which looked more like muscle than fat to her. "I've got to watch my girlish figure, you know."

"Thanks. It looks great." She grinned as she spooned scrambled eggs with cheese and some of the grits onto her plate.

Dylan scooped several large dollops of eggs and added bacon and sausage.

Billy balanced a milk carton, a butter plate, and a coffee-filled carafe as he walked back to the kitchen island. He sat and began loading his own plate.

A voice called from the other room. "What smells so good?" A short woman walked into the kitchen. When she saw Dylan her eyes widened, but then a huge grin covered her face. She walked over to him. "Dylan, what are you doing here?"

"I came to see my favorite woman in the world. Well, favorite, after my mama." He jumped off the stool, bent down and hugged her, then turned back to Reggie. "This is Theresa. Billy Clyde's wife."

"And my nutritionist." Billy laughed.

"What's that supposed to mean?" Theresa reached up, patted Dylan's cheek, then laughed. While Billy was a bear of a man, Theresa was the opposite of him, petite and slim, with a short haircut that had reddish blonde highlights mixed in with the brown. Her hot pink pajamas and white fluffy slippers completed the picture.

Another stereotype gone. Reggie assumed Billy Clyde, the computer nerd, lived alone in the middle of nowhere, with no social graces. Wrong again. Instead, he had an adorable-looking wife.

Theresa hugged Billy. She turned and looked at the mountain of food on the counter. She looked back at her husband and raised an eyebrow. "If I'm your nutrionist, that doesn't look like my recommendation."

"Sure it does, hon. There's the eggs and the multi-grain bread, and I even have grits." He held out his plate.

"Yeah, topped with enough butter to kill a cow." She turned to Dylan. "He's got high cholesterol. He's fighting the doctor and me on what he should and shouldn't eat."

She picked up the plate of bacon and sausage.

"That's for our guests. Not for me." Billy said with a sheepish smile. He looked down at his plate. "I don't have any idea how those got on my plate, hon. Monroe, must have done it while I was looking at your breathtaking beauty."

"What brings you here?" Theresa asked, and then laughed at her husband as she hopped on stool and looked at Dylan.

After a quick recap, they settled in for breakfast. As they ate, they discussed Reggie's dilemma.

"It sounds surreal. You have no idea who's trying to kill you or why?" Theresa asked.

"Not one." Reggie admitted. "I haven't been working long enough to get any real enemies. Plus, I'm only an assistant at this point. The firm insists all new attorneys intern for a full year."

"I couldn't believe they found us in Pennsylvania at the motel." Dylan said. "The only way they could was to have access to Reggie's credit card information. I thought you might be able to help us out with that one."

"I can find out who was looking at her credit records but it still might not tell us what we need to know." Billy nodded. "But who knows, we might be blessed with information."

"Are you telling me you not only can access my credit records, but you can find out who else has been looking at them?" Reggie stared from Dylan to Billy.

"Just like that." Billy snapped his fingers. He took his empty plate to the sink and walked back. He picked up the ketchup bottle and butter. "That'll be the easy part."

Theresa stood and collected the dirty dishes. "Hey, Dylan, how's the no smoking thing going?"

"Well," He drew the word out into two syllables. "After being shot at, knocked over the head, and a bomb on my truck, I had a moment of weakness and bought a pack at the motel. But thanks to Reggie, I resisted."

"She threw them away?" Theresa laughed and clapped. "Bravo. I guess if you can get through all that without a cigarette, you can get through anything."

"Guess so." Dylan pushed out his chest. "I am now officially a non-smoker." He pulled out a pack of gum and offered it to the group. They all started laughing. Dylan asked, "What's so funny?"

"I'll help clean up. The food was terrific, Billy. Thanks, I really needed it." Reggie looked at Theresa. "I have Type One diabetes."

"That's not good. With all that's been going on, I can't imagine you've been eating right."

Theresa stacked the dirty dishes on top of each other beside the sink.

"Theresa's a registered nurse. She says I'm her favorite patient." Billy puffed out his chest.

Theresa snorted and gave him a look. "Billy Clyde, you're my *only* patient, except when I volunteer at the hospital two days a week." Theresa turned on the hot water, spraying dish soap into the sink. After loading the dirty dishes, she turned back to Reggie. "I quit my full time job when we moved out here.

Billy and Dylan made their way to the basement. "She's gonna love having someone else to fuss over." Billy shouted over his shoulder. "Reggie, come down after Theresa gives you the lecture I know is coming."

Theresa playfully slammed the door to the basement. Folding her arms, she gave a *tsk, tsk* and shook her head at Reggie. "Girl, you've got to take care of yourself. Stress, plus diabetes, equals disaster."

"It's kind of hard to reduce stress when someone is trying to kill you."

"That it is, young lady. That it is."

20

Reggie walked down the stairs to the basement. Several steps from the bottom she froze as she scanned the enormous space. The basement had to be at least twice the size of the main floor.

Billy watched her with a lopsided grin, obviously proud of his playground.

Gone was the quaintness of the log cabin above and in its stead, an ultra-modern living space had appeared as if by magic. One corner housed a workout area complete with treadmill, weight machines and other instruments of torture. Opposite the gym, the largest TV screen she'd ever seen was attached to the wall, and eight black leather recliners formed a semicircle in front of the monstrosity, as if waiting for the movie to start.

"Would you like to see my office?" Billy asked. He motioned to a wall made entirely of glass that divided the fun side from the work side of the basement.

Reggie gawked at his office then back at the man. Who was he? His office made the computer system at Benton and Greene appear archaic. "That's your office?" It looked more like the set of a James Bond movie. "It's a bit more elaborate than I expected."

"I warned you he was a computer nerd."

Dylan walked up beside her. "I wasn't exaggerating."

"I see that."

As Billy approached the glass door leading to his office, the door slid open. Fluorescent lighting turned the office area into a glittering crystal-white room. Four large flat screen monitors hung side by side at eye level. Two walls contained computers that stretched from floor to ceiling. Red, green and amber lights flickered on the monitors. She had never seen so many computers in one place.

Reggie arched an eyebrow at her host. "What exactly is it that you do for a living, Billy?"

"I'm a consultant."

"For…"

"I could tell you, but then I'd have to kill you." He looked at Dylan and both men laughed.

"He's joking, sort of. He works for the government. That's why he lives here in Paw Paw. It may look as if it's in the middle of nowhere, but in reality it's less than a two hour drive to the most powerful city in the world, and much less by boat."

"Not to mention by helicopter." Billy added.

"You have a helicopter?" Reggie asked.

"Nah, they usually just send one for me."

"Is he kidding?" She turned to Dylan.

"About the helicopter?" Dylan shrugged. "Beats me."

Looking at the equipment for a moment, her mind took a leap. With narrowed eyes, she looked back at Billy. "Are you a spy? Is that what you're trying to tell me?"

"A spy?" Billy hooted. "I'm just good at computers and the government values my expertise."

Reggie held up a hand. "Don't tell me anymore. I don't think I want to know."

****

Sweat poured off Reggie as she turned the treadmill's speed control up another notch. It felt good to release some of the pent-up energy. She watched Dylan and Billy hunched over a computer.

Billy looked up from the keyboard and motioned for her. She grabbed a towel along the way and wiped off her face.

"Got it." Billy told her.

"Who is it?"

"A company called Millennium Marketing accessed both your credit card records and Dylan's yesterday."

"How would they know about Dylan?"

"They probably tracked him down through that rusty old thing he calls a truck." Billy explained. "When you paid for the motel rooms with your credit card, it alerted them. Good thing the two of you went shopping."

"Who are they, and why do they want to kill me?" she asked, still breathless.

"I doubt if Millennium Marketing wants to kill you. I'm doing a computer check on Millennium now. In the meantime, I need to ask you some questions."

She nodded as she wiped sweat from her face.

Dylan walked over to a small refrigerator tucked away in the corner of the room and brought her a bottle of water.

She smiled her thanks. He was so thoughtful.

"And this would be a good time for me to take a shower and maybe a short nap. That way you can talk in private," Dylan told them as he handed her the water.

"You don't have to do that. I trust you."

He patted her shoulder. "Thanks but I'm exhausted after driving all night. I've got to get some rest or I won't be of any help." He looked at Billy. "Same room as always?"

Billy nodded. "Good night, Sleeping Beauty."

After Dylan left, Reggie sat in the chair beside Billy. She wanted to ask about Dylan, but knew it wasn't the time or place.

As Billy opened a word processor, he looked at her. "Let's start at the beginning. Full name, address, social security number, place of employment"

He typed as she gave him the information. "Any brothers and sisters?"

She shook her head. She dreaded the next question.

"Parents' names?"

She told him the story of being abandoned at the age of four and the ensuing foster homes.

"You weren't ever adopted?"

"Nobody wants a little girl with diabetes. Too much work."

He looked at her for a moment but said nothing. "Do you know your parents' names?"

She nodded. "But I can't see how they would

have anything to do with what's going on."

"You just never know. People are strange creatures. Some very insignificant event for one person could be catastrophic for another. Maybe you turned down a boy for the homecoming dance, and he's waited for years to get back at you."

"If you'd known me in high school, you'd know just how wrong you are. Believe me, I was very forgettable." She laughed. "My mother's name was…is…" Reggie shrugged. "Her name is Jeannie Myers. Stanley Federer is listed as the father on my birth certificate."

He stared at her for a moment. "Unusual name. Do you know anything about him?"

"No, as far as I know he might have been a one night stand or they might still be together. I have no idea."

"I'm surprised you never looked them up. The Internet makes it easy."

She bit her lip. Her foot tapped against the floor, and shrugged away the painful memories of rejection. "My parents didn't want me, so I certainly wasn't going to impose myself on them. I don't need them. I can take care of myself."

Billy nodded. "I don't blame you for being angry, but it's hard to know the truth in situations like—"

"I'm not angry. I got over that a long time ago." After that, she gave him the names of all the foster parents and children she could remember, any significant relationships in her life, college experiences and anything else she thought might be important.

"Almost finished." He stretched his massive arms to full length. "Do you have any idea where your parents lived when they deserted you?"

"Not really. I always assumed Philadelphia, since that's where I grew up, but I don't really know. The social workers would never tell me who my parents were. I didn't learn that until I became an adult. By that time, I didn't care to learn any more about them."

He nodded and looked back at the monitor. Using the cursor, he reviewed the information. He stared at her for a moment. "Don't take the next questions personally, but I gotta ask."

She nodded.

"Any bad habits I need to know about—drugs or gambling? Anything that might bring you into contact with the darker side of life?"

"No way. Never had the time. Too busy working and going to school."

"Did you use any creative ways to help with paying for college that might have been on the wrong side of the law? You know a lot of people do."

"I didn't have to." She shook her head and tried not to feel insulted. He was helping her. "Pennsylvania has some sort of fund for foster children so they can go to college if their grades are good enough. I made sure mine were good enough."

"Good for you. That's enough for now." Billy stood. "Let me show you where you can take a shower and rest. You're probably tired, too."

"I am but I slept some in the truck. Dylan did all the driving."

"So Sundance, how long have you and Butch been running from the outlaws?"

"I met Dylan...*Butch* last Wednesday—" So began the crazy story of the past few days. "Have you ever heard anything so crazy? I crash into him and he invites me to his house for a holiday dinner. Not to mention, I have someone out to kill me and he drives me halfway across the country to a computer geek friend—no offense."

Billy threw his head back and barreled out a laugh. "Reggie, If I wasn't one-hundred percent, totally and completely in love with Theresa, I'd marry you!"

"Dylan is amazing and the most caring person in the world."

"That's Monroe. He believes God orchestrates everything and has called him to help those in need. Whatever the need may be."

"Why would anyone put themselves into danger for a stranger?" She looked at Billy. "Don't you think that's a little off the wall?"

"Not really, that's pretty much my philosophy, too."

She didn't get it. Sure, the police and firefighters did that, but they got paid to do it. "I can understand doing it to protect someone you love, but not someone you don't even know."

"You aren't a Christian, are you?"

"What's that got to do with it?"

"Everything."

21

A strange bed. A strange room. Again.

Reggie stretched and glanced at her watch. Her four hour nap had done a world of good. In spite of feeling better physically, the reality of her situation overwhelmed her. She hadn't felt this helpless in a long time.

However, hope glimmered in the forms of Dylan, Billy, and Theresa. She'd been lucky enough to meet three of the kindest people in the world. Two former Marines and a nurse. That counted for something—actually, a lot.

As crazy as it seemed, crashing into Dylan's truck had kept her alive. Weird.

She put on the new clothes Theresa had picked out. Not bad. The jeans fit perfectly and even though she'd never choose a leopard print shirt, it didn't look half bad.

After brushing her hair, Reggie tested her glucose level with a new meter Theresa had given her. She looked at the results and smiled. No problem.

She walked to the window, pulled back the heavy drapes and peered outside. Trees, trees, and more trees. How could Theresa be happy living in the middle of nowhere?

Reggie shrugged and went to find the others.

Dylan, Theresa and Billy were sitting in a semi-circle on the sofa holding hands with heads bowed when she walked into the living room. She came to an abrupt stop.

Dylan looked up. His blue eyes twinkled and his smiled welcomed her. "It's OK, Reggie. We're just praying and asking for God's protection and guidance."

She nodded as if she heard such words on a regular basis, which couldn't be further from the truth. The group dropped hands and Billy stared at her for so long she wondered if she'd grown red horns while brandishing a three-pronged pitchfork.

He motioned her to take a seat.

"I found out a few things, but let's take it one step at a time. Are you sure you don't know any other information about your father?"

That wasn't what she expected. She shook her head. Why did he want to know about her father?

"Have you ever heard of Stanley Software?" Dylan asked.

"Of course, everyone has." Stanley Software was the king of computer software.

"The owner's name is Stanley Federer." Billy said.

She let the words sink in for a moment and then rejected the implication. "Surely, you don't think it's the same man listed on my birth certificate?"

"I'm thinking it is. Stanley Software's headquarters is right outside of Philadelphia."

"Yeah, but—" What a ridiculous idea. Her father the founder of Stanley Software. No way.

"Billy Clyde accessed their human resource files and found out that a Jeannie Meyers worked there as a receptionist twenty-five years ago." Dylan looked at her.

"You think the owner of Stanley Software is my biological father?"

"All the information seems to say yes. I know it's hard to believe." Billy nodded. "As far as I could find out, Pennsylvania has no college scholarship program like you described but Stanley Software instituted one for needy students in foster care. It started seven years ago—just the time you graduated from high school."

"So you're telling me my biological father is the billionaire, Stanley Federer?"

He lifted a group of papers and showed them to her. "Your name is listed as one of the recipients for the first year of the program." He took a deep breath. "Here's another thing. Millennium Marketing, the company watching your credit cards, is a subsidiary of Stanley Software."

****

Dylan watched Reggie as she processed Billy Clyde's information. The struggle showed on her face.

"You think my father is trying to kill me?" Her voice trembled when she spoke.

He fought the urge to hug her. If he could make all her pain go away, he would.

"It's a possibility, but I don't really think so." Billy Clyde paced around the room before turning back to Reggie. "Why would he arrange a scholarship for you and then hire a hit man seven years later? Doesn't make sense."

"You're right. That doesn't make sense." Her voice was hopeful, like a six-year-old who didn't want her parents to be angry.

Dylan felt the urge to protect her. Even though Reggie claimed she wanted nothing to do with her biological father, he couldn't imagine how shocking it would be to think one's own father was trying to kill one.

"So, what do you think is going on, hon?" Theresa asked.

"Let's look at this logically. Why are most murders committed?" Billy wandered over to the candy dish and grabbed a handful of chocolate covered candies. He popped several in his mouth, in spite of Theresa's disapproving scowl.

"Well according to the mysteries I read, love or money," Theresa answered. "Move away from the candy dish, hon."

Billy looked down at his hand. His face registered surprise. He sat down on the sofa and popped the last of the candy in his mouth.

"Or revenge." Dylan chimed in. He looked over at Reggie. Her foot tapped a nervous beat against the couch.

"That's the way I see it. Love, money, or revenge. Which one of those do you think you fits, Reggie?" Billy asked.

Dylan walked over and grabbed his own handful of candy, then sat on the armrest of Reggie's chair. He rested his hand on her shoulder. "The man is worth billions. It's probably all of the above."

"Good point." Theresa said. "All this cloak and dagger intrigue has made me hungry. Let's grill some steaks and we can chew on the information along with our dinner."

"That's the best advice I've heard all day." He bowed to Theresa. "Oh, wise wife. I've got my computer doing a search on Mr. Federer as we speak. It should be done by the time we finish eating."

"Good." Theresa glared first at Billy, then at Dylan. She stood and walked towards the kitchen. "Reggie you and I will start dinner while James Bond and Q wash up and put away their spy toys."

Theresa squealed as Billy Clyde chased her into the kitchen. They were true partners in every sense of the word.

Something Dylan wanted more than anything. Someone to share his life with.

He wanted it. And he wanted Reggie.

You're a fool Monroe. What would a lawyer see in a farmer? You're dreamin, man. But, oh, what a dream!

22

The scent of grilled steak wafted into the kitchen, making Reggie's mouth water in anticipation. Holding the knife in mid-air, she paused from chopping green peppers and glanced at the beautiful woman preparing the dinner table. "I love your outfit."

Theresa wore an African-inspired pantsuit with reds, yellows, and oranges swirled together with just a touch of blue. Her shoes matched the blue in the material perfectly. She looked as if she'd just stepped off a photo shoot, rather than cooking dinner in a log cabin in Paw Paw, West Virginia.

"Thanks." Theresa stirred the sizzling vegetables with a spatula. "Dylan's a good man. You're blessed to have him by your side."

Reggie's gaze strayed to the men outside, grilling steaks. "I would be dead if not for him." She looked up at Theresa. "We've been through so much together. It is hard to remember my life without him in it." Scraping the green peppers and onions into the salad bowl, Reggie's pulse increased. *I don't want my old life back, I want a life with Dylan.* Could it really work? A country boy and city girl? And what about his faith in God? She wasn't even sure there *was* a God. "And he's cute." Reggie giggled.

"You better believe it, girl."

Reggie concentrated on cutting up the tomatoes and cucumbers for the salad. "Theresa, can I ask you something?"

"Sure, you can." Theresa smiled.

"Do you like living out here? It feels so remote and you seem more like a city girl to me."

Theresa turned off the burner and removed the wok from the stove. After stirring the rice, she turned back to Reggie. "If you're asking if I prefer city life, I do. But I love making my husband happy even more, and living out here makes him happy. So, here I am."

"But what about you? Don't you regret giving up your own life, your own career?"

"Oh, I am living my life the way I want." Theresa spoke softly. "I couldn't be happy anywhere without Billy, but I can be happy anywhere with him."

"You must love him a lot to live out here. I don't think I could do it."

"We have a great life together. We have friends from church. I volunteer at the school as a nurse. If you stay out here long enough Reggie, you'll fall madly in love with this place. There is something to be said about being surrounded with God's majestic and beautiful creation." Theresa pulled out two bowls from the knotty pine cabinets. "And when I get lonely, I go visit our kids in Nashville."

"How many children do you have?"

"Two, a boy, and a girl, and three amazing grandchildren." She spooned out the rice in a serving bowl. "Billy has it set up so we can video call them. It's the next best thing to being there."

"Grandchildren? You aren't old enough for that." Reggie finished cutting the vegetables and scooped them up and into the salad bowl.

"Don't I wish?" Theresa lifted up the wok, and using the spatula, put the stir-fry into a bowl.

"Why don't you live in Nashville?"

"Billy needs to be near DC for his job. So, this is my home for now."

Reggie gathered up the knife and cutting board, and took them to the sink. "It almost looks like a national forest."

"It only seems that way." Theresa laughed. "We live at the edge of a state park. We only own a few acres of land, but when you look out, it looks as if we are the only people for miles and miles."

They carried the bowls over to the table just as Dylan and Billy walked in with the steaks. Once the table was set, the group sat down. Theresa smiled at her husband. "Dylan, will you say the blessing?"

As Dylan prayed, Reggie closed her eyes. She'd never known people like this. God was truly a part of their daily life.

"The food looks great." Reggie stared at the steak on her plate for a moment. "But there's no way I can eat a serving that big."

"Do your best, and the dogs can have the rest." Billy grabbed the biggest steak off the plate, but when Theresa gave him a look, he plopped it on Dylan's plate.

"You mean the dogs Dylan's afraid of?"

Reggie asked.

"I am not afraid of them. They just don't like me, so I stay as far away from them as I can." Dylan took a bite of his steak and smacked his lips.

"Whatever. I saw the look on your face when Billy was about to bring me in the house and you thought the dogs might be in."

"Just because I'm careful doesn't mean I'm afraid. Let me tell you about Billy. One time—"

Billy shook his steak knife at Dylan. "Don't do it, Monroe. I have more stories to embarrass you than you do me. And my wife already loves me."

Reggie felt a warm glow. Billy and Theresa thought Dylan had feelings for her...she wasn't sure how she felt about that. Was this love?

"We'll just see about that."

For the next forty minutes, the men took turns outdoing each other, telling funny stories, each tale more outrageous than the one before. The women laughed and hooted, which only encouraged the men to tell another.

"Enough of this silliness." Theresa stood up with her plate in her hand. "It's time to get back to work and get this girl her life back. I like her, so you two better figure out what's going on."

"Yes, ma'am." Billy gave his wife a salute.

"Y'all go on and I'll be down after I clean up here."

"Let me help." Reggie insisted.

"I'll take care of this; you've got more important things to focus on at the moment." She shooed them off with the look.

"She's serious, Reggie. Let's go." Dylan

grabbed Reggie's hand and they walked down the steps.

Warm tingles spread up her arm. Just being with Dylan made her happy.

23

With every passing moment, Reggie became more attracted to the handsome man who held her hand. She'd thought him to be a simple farmer, but time proved that notion wrong. His deep blue eyes penetrated her soul, his touch made her tingle, and his smile made her heart flutter. And no matter how many times her mind told her they had no future, her heart said otherwise.

Reggie took her hand back from Dylan's as they reached the bottom of the steps. She had to put Dylan out of her mind and focus on finding who wanted her dead and why.

Billy Clyde walked out of his office with the results of the computer search on Stanley Federer. Billy pointed at the black recliners. "We might as well get comfortable. This is going to take a while to sort through."

Reggie sat down and Dylan plopped on the arm of her recliner. His hand rested on hers.

"Lots of information." Billy handed part of the pile to Dylan and part to Reggie along with a couple pens

Dylan tousled her hair and moved to his own chair.

Billy kept the larger part for himself. "Mark anything that might be of interest and set it apart.

After we've gone through this, we'll see what we have."

Reggie focused on the articles. Most dealt with software developments or business, nothing relating to her present predicament.

At one point, she stopped to watch Billy.

He was a speed reader. Page after page, he would glance at them for a few moments and move on to the next. How did he do that? Could he teach her? That would be great when she researched a case.

By the time they'd finished, Theresa rejoined them. She plopped on Billy's lap, wrapped her arms around his neck and kissed him.

Reggie's face grew warm and her attention flitted around the room until her gaze landed on Dylan. He watched the loving couple with a smile.

With her arms still around Billy's neck, Theresa looked over at them. "Time to get to work. Let's write down the pertinent facts and see what happens."

After giving Billy one more kiss, she left his lap and walked into his office. She returned with a stack of index cards and three different colored pens on a TV tray. She sat in the black chair nearest Billy.

Billy leaned over and stage whispered to Reggie. "She has a system. Believe me it makes no sense to anyone, but I'll tell you her colored markers have helped me more than once."

"Tell me what you learned." Theresa ordered.

Reggie, Dylan and Billy began relaying the facts. Depending on business, family, or social, she wrote the facts in red, blue or black ink.

"His personal worth is 2 billion, more if you include the business."

"He may be dying. This article said he was being treated for colon cancer."

"His wife died in a car accident ten years ago."

"He has two younger sisters, but his parents are dead."

The list got longer while Theresa filled her index cards.

"He has two sons."

"He has a philanthropic foundation."

"Hold up a minute," Reggie said. "Did you say he has two sons?"

"That's what this article says." Dylan held up a paper.

Reggie held up one of her own. "This one says he has two sons and a daughter."

Theresa wrote a big question mark in red and set that card aside. "Anyone have anything else about the children? What are the names?"

After staring into space for a moment, Billy said, "The two boys names are Stanley Junior, and Stuart. I didn't see anything about a daughter, either. I'll do another search specific to his children."

When the group had exhausted their information, Dylan spoke up. "It doesn't take a genius to figure out that if the Federers are involved in this mess, it's probably about the money."

"It certainly seems that way, but how could I be a threat to them. Until now I didn't even have a clue my about my biological family." Reggie's head throbbed. "All of them are involved in any number of charities. Nothing to indicate they want to kill me."

Theresa sighed. "I agree. The only thing that links your troubles with them is the fact that Millennium Marketing is a subsidiary of Stanley Software and that might not mean anything."

"Yeah, but that's a biggie." Dylan pointed out. "I know you don't want to think it's them, but we can't rule them out."

How did he know what she wanted? How could he imagine what she was feeling? Until a few hours ago, she'd assumed her father was a deadbeat dad who'd ignored her rather than fulfill his responsibilities.

"I'm not ruling them out, but it's a lot to swallow. And I couldn't care less if it's my family who's trying to kill me. It's not like I know them," Reggie snapped. As soon as the words popped out, she regretted her outburst. Her face heated with embarrassment. She took a deep breath. "I'm sorry. I didn't mean to sound so snarky."

Theresa hugged her. "You don't need to apologize. You're under a lot of stress."

"That's no excuse to be rude, especially to all of you."

"I say go to the source." Dylan looked at Billy. "I think we should have a chat with Mr. Federer."

"Are you nuts?" Theresa and Reggie said at the same time.

"I didn't say that you should have a chat with him. You're going to stay put right here, while I go have a chat with him." Dylan said.

"Do you think you're just going to drive to

Philadelphia and walk right up to the president of Stanley Software?" Reggie asked.

He looked at Billy Clyde. "Genius and I will figure something out, right?"

Billy smiled like the Cheshire cat. "You know I hate when you call me that." Billy shook a finger at Dylan.

"I wish I could call Alexis. Maybe she found something." Reggie stood and stretched.

Billy tossed her his cell phone.

"Are you sure? I thought we didn't want them to track us."

"No way they're gonna track that phone." Billy told her with pride and confidence in his voice.

Reggie's eyes narrowed as she looked at Billy. "I think you really are a spy."

24

Reggie sat out on the deck alone, taking a moment to calm herself before she called Alexis. Trees formed a protective barrier around Billy and Theresa's property. Off to her right, dogs barked in the kennel near a small weathered barn. A breeze rustled the brown leaves on a broken corn stalk from the past summer's garden.

Taking a deep breath, she drank in the serenity. No wonder Billy lived out here. In spite of all her tension, the quiet beauty soothed her soul. Dylan was right when he said nature drew one closer to God. She smiled. It had been a long time since she thought about God, but sitting here amidst the beauty she could almost feel Him.

Unfortunately, beyond the pine trees, someone wanted her dead.

Even with the assurances no one would be able to trace the call, Reggie's hands shook as she dialed Alexis. As soon as Alexis heard Reggie's voice, she started crying. Reggie joined her. When the tears finished, Reggie took control of the conversation.

"Did you find anything?"

"We did. Do you remember the Jordan case?"

The memory came rushing back. Several months before, the police arrested Danny Jordan on a simple case of drug possession, but an overzealous Reggie demanded a DNA test to prove Danny hadn't touched the drugs. The DNA test did indeed prove a setup, but it also showed he'd committed a string of bank robberies in the area. Needless to say, Danny Jordan had been less than happy.

"Now I do." How could she have forgotten Danny Jordan? She'd almost lost her job over him.

"He was released two weeks ago. The prosecutor failed to ask for a continuance. The defense didn't waive the right of a speedy trial. The judge dismissed the case."

Reggie shook her head. Things like this disillusioned the public with the criminal justice system, and who could blame them. "What an idiot."

"I'll say, but there's more. His cellmate swears Danny told him he would get even with you."

"Even with me? I informed him of my plan. He should have stopped me, but he knew he hadn't touched those drugs. Not my fault he knew about the robberies and I didn't."

"Yeah, well no one ever said criminals were smart."

Reggie stood and paced the deck. Finally, she understood. Ridiculous reasoning on Danny's part, but she'd known the threat didn't have anything to do with her father. It was time to get back to her life. Or at least she could, after they found Danny. "What are the police doing about it?"

"They're looking for him, but haven't been able to locate him yet. According to his mother, he left town a few days ago, but who knows?"

A few days ago, just when all her troubles started. It all made sense. Reggie's foot tapped against the picnic table's leg. "What do they want me to do?"

"As soon as he's in custody, you can come back. They expect to find him sometime today. They have several leads, according to Ray."

"Oh, you've been in contact with Officer Ray, have you?" It felt good to tease Alexis rather than dwell on her problems. .

"Don't start it, Reg." Alexis giggled. "And just so you know, as soon as they get him in custody, Officer Ray and I are going to celebrate his capture with an official first date."

"Terrific. I'm so glad my troubles helped you get a date." After they finished laughing, Reggie hung up. Her gaze turned towards the heavens. Maybe, God was out there after all, watching out for her. She'd never felt she had a Protector before.

Reggie walked back into the house, only to find Dylan and Billy hunched over a chessboard, arguing over a move. Theresa sat beside her husband with a book in her hand. She looked up and smiled at Reggie.

"I can go home." Reggie announced. As she told them what she'd learned from Alexis, she saw the men exchange glances with each other.

"What?" she demanded. "What was that look about?"

"It just seems a little odd to me." Dylan shrugged. "You think this Danny Jordan could access your information through Millennium Marketing, and that he had car bombs and bugging devices?"

Billy frowned, but nodded his agreement. He opened the laptop sitting beside the chessboard and started typing.

"I don't know." She didn't want to agree with them. She wanted to go home and put this nightmare behind her. "I agree it sounds a bit farfetched, but then again, it's ridiculous to think my father wants me killed. He would have no reason. And we don't even know if he's my father." She sighed and sank into a nearby easy chair, her momentary jubilation gone.

"Mmm. Here's an interesting coincidence." Billy looked up from the notebook computer. "Millennium Marketing does have an office in Cleveland. So, it's possible that Danny-boy might know someone who accessed the information for him."

Closing the book, Theresa looked up at her husband. "So, what are you saying, hon? You don't think it was a professional hit? Just some scumbag trying to get revenge?"

"It's a possibility. I'd feel a lot better if they had Danny-boy in custody."

"Same here." Dylan agreed.

"It does seem like an odd coincidence, doesn't it?" Reggie shrugged. "But stranger things have happened."

Theresa stood and walked towards the kitchen. "Reggie, why don't you call the Cleveland Police? Maybe they'll convince you that it was this guy, or that it wasn't. Not to mention they might want to know about what happened at the motel."

"Good idea. Let me go find the card Officer

Ray gave me."

****

After a long discussion with Officer Davis, Reggie walked outside. Dylan, Theresa, and Billy had congregated on the deck to watch the sunset. She pinched her coat closely against her neck as the wind blew through her hair. Dylan grabbed her hand and pulled her onto his lap.

Theresa and Billy held hands. Theresa hummed a song Reggie didn't recognize. The last remnants of the sun slipped into darkness. The tall, thin trees stuck up from the ground like match sticks from the glow of the moon and the twinkling of the stars.

Leaning back against Dylan, she stared up at the twinkling stars, savoring the moment.

"What's the verdict?" Dylan broke the silence.

"He's in custody and they're convinced it was him even though he's denying everything."

"Now, that's a big surprise." Theresa said.

"Just to be on the safe side, they're going to do some checking into the motel break-in, but I've been given a green light to go back home." Reaching past Dylan, Reggie set the cell phone on the table. "They were very curious about why your phone number didn't register on their system."

"I'm sure they were." Billy chuckled. "What did you tell them?"

"What do you think? I told them that I could tell them, but then I'd have to kill them."

"I've taught you well." Billy gave her a

thumbs up.

Dylan hooted.

"Actually, I told them I had no idea. I suggested maybe they should have a technician look at their system."

That made the men laugh even harder.

Theresa looked over at Reggie and rolled her eyes. "Men are such strange creatures, aren't they? So, what happens now?"

Dylan looked at Reggie. "Ready to go home?"

"Absolutely. I can stay with Alexis until I get new furniture." She pressed her hands into a praying position. "Finally, the whole ugly nightmare's over."

"I hope." Dylan sounded doubtful. "I'm just not as sure about this Danny Jordan character as the police. It seems a bit too convenient to me."

"If they look hard enough, they'll probably find a connection between him and Millennium Marketing," Billy said. He smiled at Reggie. "I'm glad you'll be able to put this behind you."

Looking around the table, it sounded to Reggie as if all of them were trying to convince themselves everything was fine. For just a moment, she had an uneasy feeling, but quickly dismissed it. She wanted to go home.

"What are you going to do about Stanley Federer?" Theresa asked.

"Nothing. What's there to do?" Reggie got a little flustered.

"You know he paid for your college education. That should count for something. It shows he cares about you." Dylan stood and moved to the edge of the deck. "He might be thrilled if you contacted him."

"You can explain that you found out about the college money and you wanted to call to thank him." Billy said.

"It could break the ice between the two of you," Dylan added.

Reggie looked at the group and shook her head. "You are all hopeless romantics or hopeless optimists. Either way, it's not going to happen. I'm sure he paid for my college to ease his conscience." She thought for a moment. "He's known where I was all along. He could have contacted me any time he wanted to."

"True." Billy nodded. "Back to the issue at hand, it would be prudent to be careful for the next few weeks."

"Stop looking for trouble." Reggie told him. "With your imagination, maybe you should write murder mysteries."

"Sure, why not? It's not like he's all that busy, working for the government and everything." Dylan laughed.

"Don't forget, to add business owner to the list."

Reggie stared at her host. "You're kidding, right?"

"No, I was tired of hearing my kids complain about the lack of good software for their children so I started up a little company in my spare time."

Reggie walked over to where the big man stood. She crooked her finger and he bent down. She hugged him. "Thanks for all your help. I just want to go home and forget any of this ever happened."

25

Reggie stepped out of the truck and was met with a hug from Dylan's sister. Reggie noticed Joni's red eyes and nose, but said nothing. Maybe, she'd had a fight with Richard about Reggie staying the night.

After the long drive, she certainly couldn't insist Dylan drive her back to Cleveland. He'd been the one who suggested she stay over with his sister again, but she hadn't meant to cause a problem. She would visit for a minute and then call a cab to take her back to Alexis's apartment.

"You two are going to be the death of me. I couldn't believe it when you called me from West Virginia and told me what happened. Mom said you had to go out of town, but not why." Joni went from one to the other hugging them. "I had no idea."

"We're fine, sis. Just a little tired. What's wrong with you?"

She looked away for a moment, but turned back with a smile. "Nothing. I'm just glad you two—"

"Don't tell me nothing. With a nose like Rudolph. That means you've either been crying, or eating hot peppers."

"I never could hide anything from you." She

hugged her brother. "We're drowning in bills. Richard's hours were cut at the factory again. We're going to be a little short this month, but we'll get by."

"God has a way of providing." Dylan assured her.

Joni sighed. "I know. I know. I just wish He'd let me in on the plan, especially with Christmas coming."

"I could use some help on the farm." Dylan offered.

"Liar. The last thing you need is another farm hand in the winter." Joni punched her brother. "Forget it, we'll manage. Let's eat. I've got some food ready. Everyone else is at the evening service so it will be quiet."

Joni bustled around her kitchen while Reggie and Dylan took turns telling her about the past few days. Dylan grabbed a piece of fried chicken as soon as she set the platter in front of him. Along with the chicken were mashed potatoes, noodles, and broccoli.

"I can't believe what you've been through. It must have been horrible." Looking at Reggie, Joni shook her head.

"It was bad, but thanks to Dylan, I lived through it." Reggie's eyes filled with tears and she patted Dylan's hand. "You have an amazing brother."

"That's my baby brother. I'm so proud of him."

"Let's end this meeting of my fan club," Dylan told them as he scooped a second helping of noodles on his plate.

"And humble, too." Joni jumped up and hugged Reggie. "I'm so glad everything turned out OK and that you're safe. You can have our room again."

"But—"

"No arguing. I know you're exhausted and no reason to go back to your apartment tonight. Are you going to show her the farm tomorrow?"

Dylan shrugged. "I hadn't thought about it." He looked over at Reggie.

"Sounds fun." Reggie nodded.

Dylan had been so wonderful to her, the least she could do was to show interest in his life.

"Good, we'll come over after I get the kids off to school." Joni stood and began to clear the dishes.

"I guess that's my hint that it's time to go." Dylan stood.

"Such a smart boy, you are." Joni winked at Reggie who laughed.

As Dylan was leaving, Reggie watched brother and sister hugging each other. It was obvious how much they loved each other. What would it have been like to have a brother or a sister growing up? It occurred to her, if Billy was right about Stanley Federer, she did have siblings. She brushed away the thought. Stanley Federer's family had nothing to do with her.

"I'll give you a moment." Joni smiled and walked back in the kitchen, leaving Dylan and her alone.

"Dylan, I don't know—"

He took a step towards her and her pulse raced. "Don't say it. I'm glad I could help." He leaned down and his lips brushed her cheek, leaving a tingle in their wake. "See you in the morning." He turned and walked out the door.

When Reggie walked in the kitchen, Joni wiped tears from her eyes with the corner of her apron.

"You must hate me for putting Dylan in so much danger the past few days." Reggie couldn't blame her.

"Not in the least, Reggie." She sputtered a denial. "God knew Dylan was the man to protect you, and besides Dylan's never been one to play it safe. A warrior needs adventures from time to time."

"Dylan told me about Daniella."

"He took it so hard. He felt as if he should have known, but she didn't tell us. It took a long time for him to come to terms with the fact it wasn't his fault."

"I think it's part of the reason, he's determined to keep me safe."

"And besides, God brought the two of you together for a reason."

"That's what I keep hearing." Reggie said with a smile.

"Tell me about your faith, or is that too personal of a question?"

She didn't have any to speak of, and it was hard to admit that to Joni. "It's not, but what I'd really like is to go out and look at some of your art, if that's not too personal."

"Touché." Joni laughed. "Aren't you too tired?"

"I need to unwind a bit if I'm ever going to get

to sleep."

Joni squeezed her hand. "Well, if you need something to make you sleepy, my painting might be just the thing."

****

Reggie punched her pillow. As exhausted as she was, her mind wouldn't slow down enough to let sleep come. Finally, she gave up and let her thoughts drift. It took only a moment for them to land on Dylan.

She'd never met a man like him before. She thought he was a simple farmer, but he was so much more than that. Sweet, funny, and smart, and he'd risked his life for her without a second thought. And hadn't even tried to get her into bed.

A part of her screamed to go for it, but the more practical part listed the reasons why a relationship would never work. He would never fit in with her lifestyle. Her friends would think him crazy when he started talking about God. Her face flushed with embarrassment. Her friends wouldn't understand...she sighed. She didn't know what to think.

In spite of the horror of the weekend, she'd met some wonderful people. Dylan, his family, Billy Clyde, and Theresa. If they were what Christians were like, religion might not be such a bad thing. In fact, at the moment it seemed like a pretty good thing.

Finally, she drifted off to sleep.

26

Once the kids were off, Joni and Reggie walked out to the art studio in the back yard. "Are you sure you want to take these pictures with you? They aren't that good. Your friend might not—"

"Believe me, they are wonderful." Reggie only wished she could paint half as well. If she could, she might have chosen art over the law as a career. Jeffrey was going to love them. Hopefully, he could ease Joni and Richard's financial worries. "And I'm sure my friend can sell them. In fact, I'm going straight to his art gallery after Dylan drops me off at my car. One of the things that amazes me is the different styles you use. And you do all of them well."

"A matter of opinion but thanks for the vote of confidence." Joni's face flushed but she smiled.

Using towels to cushion them, Reggie and Joni packed five paintings into Joni's minivan, and then headed out to Dylan's farm. Turning left at the square of Fredericksburg, they passed the town's only factory. A few minutes later, they turned right and went further in the country.

Reggie studied the countryside of harvest colors from the car window. Fields of dry grass rippled over open space. Barren trees planted in narrow rows separated one field from another. It was her life. Dry and empty like the scenery before her.

Her throat burned and the tears came. *Please let Joni keep her eyes on the road.* Could she really walk away from Dylan and go back to her life in the city? How could she give up the only person she'd ever felt safe with? Ever loved. What a ridiculous thought. She' couldn't be in love; she'd only known him for a week. Her mind agreed, but her heart dissented.

It was time to get back to work, to her life. She should feel excited, but instead, she felt sick to her stomach.

They turned down a bumpy lane. Her head bounced in rhythm to the music on the radio. An old white farmhouse stood among several barns. The largest was painted red, but the others were old weathered wood. Cows stood grazing in the fields. It looked just the way she expected. Dreary.

"What kind of cows are those?"

"Dairy. Dylan has a few beef cows, but those are for personal use. He's working on a couple of other things that seem promising."

Joni pulled up beside Dylan's truck, already parked in front of the large red barn, and shut off the motor. By the time, Reggie was out of the van, Dylan was walking out of the barn and towards them, trailing some of the biggest, ugliest looking chickens Reggie had ever seen. Not that she'd seen many.

"Those turkeys are a nuisance but Dylan insists on having them and he lets them go wherever they want. But you've got to admit they do taste good."

Feeling stupid, and more than a little grateful she hadn't uttered the word chicken out loud, she nodded.

Then Joni's words sank in.

Reggie swallowed hard. "You mean we ate some of them the other day?"

"Sure."

Reggie repressed a shudder. She knew the meat she ate came from animals, but seeing them face-to-face was more intimacy than she cared for.

"Morning." Dylan wore a red plaid flannel shirt and his hair fluttered in the wind, in spite of the baseball cap he wore. He looked well-rested. He must have slept better than she had.

He turned and shooed the turkeys. They gobbled and scattered in several different directions.

"So, this is where you live?" Reggie asked, with more cheer than she felt.

"Not really. That's where the folks live. My place is on the other side of the farm."

"Mom and Dad wanted Dylan to move into the house, but he bought a manufactured home and put it on the other side so they couldn't keep track of him."

"A manufactured home?"

"Like mobile homes and double-wides." Dylan explained. "I thought about building a house, but this was easier and it took a lot less time."

He lived in a trailer. She would never be able to admit that to her friends. *You've become a snob, Reggie Myers.* Growing up, she'd have been ecstatic to have a trailer to call her own.

"Help me put these in your truck." Joni pointed at the paintings piled up on her minivan's floor. "Then I've got to be going. I've got things to do."

"Put what?" Dylan took a step towards the van.

"It's the craziest thing. Reggie thinks she can sell some of my paintings to a friend who owns an art gallery in Cleveland."

"What's so crazy about that? We've been telling you for years how talented you are."

"I don't have time to be talented. I'm a mother." She wagged a finger at Dylan.

Reggie laughed. After seeing the morning commotion at Joni's house, Reggie knew Joni spoke the truth.

After the paintings were transferred to the truck, Joni gave Reggie a big hug. "I'll be praying for you. In the meantime, don't be a stranger. You're welcome to stay with us anytime. I'll call you in a few days." Joni walked to her car and gave them a small wave as she left.

Reggie turned to Dylan. "Your sister is so sweet."

"Yes, she is, but don't tell her I said so. Do you really think you can sell her paintings?"

"Absolutely." She nodded. "Jeffrey will go bonkers over them."

"That would be great."

"In fact, after you take me back to Alexis's and my rental car, I'm just going to head straight down to his gallery."

"Mmmm. Why don't I just take you there,

myself. I'd like to hear what he has to say about them."

She looked at Dylan in his flannel shirt and old jeans, and thought of him meeting Jeffrey. She winced inwardly. The two of them would be like oil and water. "Not necessary. You've done so much already. I don't know how I'm ever going to thank you."

Dylan's eyes turned soft as he looked at her. For a moment, it was hard for Reggie to breathe. He took a step towards her, but she turned towards the barn. "Are you going to show me this farm of yours or what?"

She smiled, but she saw the hurt in his eyes.

He touched her arm. "Hold up, Reggie. We need to talk."

Her stomach clenched. Dylan was a wonderful guy, but he wasn't the guy for her. He'd been so wonderful to her, and she didn't want to hurt his feelings, but it wouldn't be right to lead him on.

"Dylan, I've been through a lot the last few da—" She pasted a smile on.

"I know and I'm not trying to make it harder for you, but I need to know."

She swallowed hard. "Need to know what?" Her gaze traveled up to meet his sweet blue eyes.

"You can't deny the attraction between us, but I'm not a lovesick teenager. I know it takes more than a little chemistry to make a relationship work. What I want to know is, do you want to take some time to explore the possibility of us? To see what happens?"

In spite of the chill of the morning, his hand

felt warm even through her coat sleeve. She longed for him to take her in his arms. To feel his lips on hers. She stepped towards him and his arms tightened around her. She laid her cheek against the softness of his flannel shirt. His heart beat softly against her.

He cupped her chin with his calloused hand and lifted her face. Their lips met with a sweetness she'd never known. The possibility of us? *He isn't talking about casual dating. He's talking about something more permanent.* Her heart fluttered in fear.

Love didn't last. You could love someone for a while, but not forever. They always left. No matter what they said or how hard you tried, they always left. Sooner or later, Dylan would leave, and then she'd be alone again.

If she gave Dylan her heart, and he left, she wouldn't be able to survive.

She laid her hands on his chest and pushed away from him. His gaze locked on hers. She knew he saw the answer.

27

Reggie drove down Euclid Avenue towards University Circle. With tissue in hand, she wiped away the tears. The drive back to Cleveland with Dylan had been uncomfortable, but in true Dylan fashion, he'd done his best to keep the tone light. To not make her feel any worse than she already did.

Another tear leaked out.

Sighing, she put on the turn signal to pass a car. The flashing green arrow beat in time with her broken heart. It reminded her of Dylan and how they'd met. More tears.

It was ridiculous to act this way. She'd known him for less than a week, and it had been her decision not to pursue a relationship. Turning her mind from Dylan, she focused on driving. Weaving through an obstacle course of construction cones and heavy traffic was a challenge.

Jeffrey had a prime location for an art gallery, just blocks from the Cleveland Museum of Art, as well as other smaller museums in the area. University Circle was the cultural center for Cleveland.

Of course, Jeffrey being Jeffrey, his gallery wasn't just an art gallery. The attached coffee house brought folks in on the weekends, and boasted the most delicious pastries. On Friday and Saturday evenings, patrons packed in to listen to poetry or music while they perused the art.

Once he'd even had a mime. It hadn't gone so well.

She pulled into the small parking lot behind the gallery and cut the engine. Every muscle screamed with tension. Wiping away the tears, she dashed on a little makeup to hide them, pasted on a smile, and stepped out of the car. Picking out her favorite painting, she headed to the back door of the gallery.

She hit the buzzer. The intercom reminded her of Billy Clyde and Theresa. Such good people.

She sighed.

"Who is it?" His voice sounded tinny coming through the intercom.

"It's Reggie." After she heard the buzz, Reggie walked through the back door. She leaned the picture against the wall. She would surprise him with it in a minute.

Jeffrey looked up from his cluttered desk in the corner of the workroom. Space was limited, so his office was shared with the frames and paintings waiting to be hung. The scent of varnish mixed with the coffee aroma from the adjoining rooms.

His chocolate brown eyes flashed a welcome as he jumped up and gave her a hug. "Thank goodness, you're here. You can rescue me from all this dreariness." His hands fluttered towards his desk. "Reggie, dear, what are you doing here on a weekday? You never take a day off. Are you sick?" He felt her forehead and frowned. "No fever."

"You wouldn't believe me if I told you, but that can wait. I wanted you to look at this painting and tell me what you think." She pointed at the picture she'd deposited by the door.

Jeffrey turned it around, but said nothing for a few minutes as he examined it with trained eyes. "It's delightful. It's whimsical and fun, but still beautiful. Who painted it?"

"Nobody you know." Reggie smiled. She knew how to push his buttons.

"Don't be so sure." He raised an eyebrow.

"Oh, I'm sure." She challenged.

Jeffrey hated it when others knew something about the art world he didn't.

"She's an artist I met over the weekend. I thought you might be interested in selling her work. I brought a few more paintings along, in case you wanted them."

"Let's take a look."

After a trip to her car, they lined Joni's paintings on easels. Jeffrey paraded back and forth in front of them, stopping to stare at each. Finally, he looked up at Reggie. His hands fluttered towards the paintings. "These are wonderful. Simply wonderful. You say she has more."

"Tons more."

"Give me her number. Perhaps, I'll arrange a show. In the meantime, I'll call a few of my special customers and give them first dibs on these."

"How much will they sell for?" Reggie hoped it would be enough to help with Joni and Richard's money woes.

Jeffrey looked back at the artwork and tapped his finger to his forehead. "I think I can get two thousand for them."

"Two thousand. That's great. That means they're four hundred each. I'll take the landscape. Go ahead and frame it for me."

He rolled his eyes and clicked his tongue. "No, no, no, my dear. I meant two thousand a piece."

"Oh, my." She blinked. That was a surprise. She'd known they were good, but that good? She thought for a moment. "I'll still take the landscape."

"You paying by check?"

"I wish. I'll have to use my credit card." She rummaged through her purse and handed it to Jeffrey."

"There's no hurry. You can pay later. I trust you."

"There is a hurry. She needs the cash but, please, don't tell her I bought the first one. She'll think it's charity. And I expect you to cut your commission. Her brother saved my life this weekend."

"Whaaat? You mean figuratively, of course."

"No, I mean literally. I had people shooting at me."

He grabbed her arm. "Do tell, girlfriend."

"I'll need a cup of coffee, first. And if I'm buying that picture for two thousand, it better be a free cup."

"Let me have Robin run your card, and I'll even throw in the framing for half price."

"You're all heart, Jeffrey."

28

Dylan shoved another stick of gum in his mouth as his truck rumbled down the highway. It was his fourth since dropping Reggie at Alexis's condo. He refused to let this get him down, or make him start smoking again. He'd just survived people shooting at him, and car bombs. He was tough enough to take Reggie's rejection.

Too bad, but better to know now, than to hurt more later. The romantic in him thought she might be the one, but no such luck.

She was right, of course. Long-distance relationships were tough. And since it was more than a two-hour drive from the farm to her condo, they wouldn't have been able to see much of each other. And she wasn't a Christian. Yet.

The gas gauge hovered on E. Time to make a pit stop. Good thing he was at the Burbank exit. He pulled up to the gas pump just as his cell phone started singing.

"Hey, Billy Clyde."

"What's happening with you, Monroe?"

"I just dropped off Reggie and am heading home."

"I was afraid of that. Someone's still watching her credit cards."

Dylan pounded his fist on the steering wheel.

"How do you know?"

"Because I'm still watching them watch her."

"Are you sure?" This wasn't any of his business any longer. She'd made that clear.

"Could be nothing, buddy, but do you want to take that chance?"

"You think Reggie's still in danger?"

"I'm saying there's a chance. Can't say for sure."

Dylan stepped out of the car and slid his debit card in the card reader and punched in his PIN. "You know if I go running back up to Cleveland and it ends up being a mistake, she's going to think I'm crazy. She'll think I'm trying to use it to get close to her again. She blew me off. You know, the bit about just being friends and all."

He lifted the gas nozzle and walked to the tank.

"It probably wouldn't have worked out, anyway." Billy said philosophically. "Way too beautiful for your ugly self."

"I know, but it hurt my man pride."

"I'm sure it did, Monroe, but your man pride isn't what's important at the moment." Billy laughed. "You might end up looking a little foolish if I'm wrong, but what if I'm not wrong?"

Dylan removed the nozzle and walked back the pump. He wouldn't turn his back on Reggie. It didn't matter if she wasn't romantically interested in him. If she needed help, he was going to help her if he could. "I'll call her and tell her what you discovered."

"Sounds like a plan. I'll be here. Call me if you need anything."

"Thanks, Billy Clyde. Good catch." He stepped back up in the truck cab.

Dylan looked up Reggie's number and hit the send button. Her voice mail came on without a ring. She had the phone shut off. Dylan tried the number again. Same results.

He left the station and pulled back on the highway, going north towards Cleveland as and tried the number multiple times. What was the point of having a cell phone if it wasn't turned on?

He called Alexis, but she hadn't heard from Reggie since the previous day.

Then, he remembered, her battery needed charging. She'd been so anxious to get to her friend's gallery, she probably hadn't bothered to take the time to fish out the charger from her luggage they picked up at the Pennsylvania motel.

He called Billy Clyde and explained the problem.

"Her credit card rang up at some place called Jeffrey's."

"Her friend's art gallery."

Billy Clyde gave him the address.

"Why don't you call the gallery and see if she's there? I'm already on my way," Dylan said.

"I'm all over it."

Dylan hit the gas and headed up the highway. He'd driven a few miles when Billy called back.

"There's no phone number listed. Just an address."

"That doesn't make sense. Why wouldn't a business have a telephone?"

"Who knows? It's probably the latest way to show they're so successful they don't really need your business."

Dylan hit the steering wheel.

"Stay calm, buddy. We're probably just overreacting."

"I hope so. Later." As he hung up, he pressed his foot down on the gas pedal.

29

Jeffrey's hands flew to his cheeks with exaggerated mock shock.

Reggie laughed. "What can I say? Some people just have exciting lives." Sitting with him felt good. Nothing to worry about. She stirred her French vanilla cappuccino and took another sip.

"I can't believe all that happened to you. Mind-boggling, simply mind-boggling, I say. And this Dylan creature sounds simply scrumptious." Jeffrey's white teeth glistened against his naturally tanned complexion. "I certainly hope you plan to pursue this gentleman."

They sat in the back of the gallery at Jeffrey's desk. Reggie sipped the last dregs of her cappuccino, no sugar—extra foam. "Actually, I don't plan. We have nothing in common." Her voice turned wistful. "It wouldn't work out."

Jeffrey clicked his teeth. "Are you kidding me? He sounds perfectly marvelous. I don't know what your problem is, girl."

"Stop being such a romantic." She rolled her eyes. "It's more complicated than the fact that he's one of the sweetest, most trust-worthy men I've ever met, not to mention sexy and good-looking."

"Oh, yeah, I can see how that would be a problem."

"Think about it. I'm a lawyer and he's a farmer. I can't live in the middle of nowhere."

He sighed theatrically. "I'm pretty sure they have lawyers down in Wayne County. Reggie dear, you can fool some people, but you can't fool me." Jeffrey stood up. "Any particular color frame you want?"

She couldn't meet his eyes. Instead, she stared down at the coffee mug. "I have no idea what you're talking about."

"Liar." He walked behind her and slung his arms around her shoulders, his voice serious. "Reggie, I know you're afraid. We're all afraid to love, sometimes. It's even scarier when you think he might be Mr. Right. But sometimes you have to take a risk and let love happen."

"Don't be silly. I barely know the man. He's just not right for me. Can you really see me with a farmer?"

"I think—"

"Forget it, don't answer that question. And about the frame, I trust you. You decide." She set her mug on the work table. "I need to get going. I've got a ton of things to do."

"I'm glad you realize I have exquisite taste. Speaking of exquisite taste, I'm going to get on my cell phone as soon as you leave and call up my best customers. I'll have those paintings sold by the end of the day or my name's not Jeffrey Barker."

"Really? That's terrific."

"I'll call Joni in a bit and start making arrangements for her show. My latest protégé is going to make a big splash in the art world, I predict."

"And you have me to thank for it."

The back door rattled. Jeffrey rolled his eyes, tossed his head diva-style. He walked over to the door and spoke through it, not unlocking it. "Sorry, you have to go around to the front."

The doorknob rattled again, even more insistent.

"I need in. Let me in." A voice yelled through the door.

"No can do. You've got to go around to the front."

"I gotta talk to you. It's important."

The two men argued through the door. Reggie looked up at Jeffrey, but his back was to her. He stood at the door, his exasperation growing.

The hairs on Reggie's neck tingled.

Déjà vu.

She was back in Alexis's apartment and the man yelled through the door for them to leave because there was a fire. If Dylan hadn't stopped the man, he would have killed her.

Her heartbeat surged. It couldn't be. She was just being paranoid. It was all over. The man was saying something about an emergency and someone was hurt.

"Fine." Jeffrey said.

She jumped up, knocking over the chair. "No, Jeffrey. Don' let him in."

Jeffrey turned towards her. His face filled with confusion, but he'd already unlocked the door. The door flew open and a short stocky man barged in. His long scraggly black hair hid most of his face, but Reggie saw the angry red scar on his throat.

Jeffrey moved in front of the man "Sorry. This is a private area. Where's the emergency?"

The man shoved Jeffrey so hard he fell to the floor. "Right here, you idiot." He pulled a gun out of his pocket. "Don't be a hero and you won't get hurt."

Staring at the gun, Reggie froze. This couldn't be happening. It was supposed to be over and this man wasn't Danny Jordan. The police were wrong.

The man pivoted towards Reggie. Her heart stopped. Her gaze focused on the long black barrel. She hated guns, but right then wished she had Dylan's. Why hadn't she let Dylan bring her here? If only Dylan were—

"You're the one I want. You've been difficult to find, but all's well that ends well, don't you think?" He laughed.

Acid churned in her stomach and bile rose in her throat. She took a deep breath. Looking past the man, she saw Jeffrey moving. *No. No. No. Stay down, don't get up.*

But Jeffrey stood.

The man's gaze met Reggie's. His mouth turned up in a cruel satisfied smile, then he swiveled, and without hesitation, pulled the trigger.

****

Dylan pulled in the parking lot. He recognized Reggie's rental car sitting there. Good, she was here. Maybe, there was no need to actually go in and make a fool of himself in front of her friend.

He could wait until she came out and explain what Billy had learned, warn her to be careful, and that would be that. Reggie wouldn't have to think of him as some sort of lovesick stalker and she could get on with her life.

A gunshot split the air, followed by Reggie screaming.

His heart thudded to a stop and his mind froze.

Grabbing his keys, he jumped out of the truck and ran to the tailgate. He shuffled through the keys until he found the right one. Adrenaline shot through him as he tore open his toolbox and seized the hidden pistol.

He slapped an ammo clip into his pistol and another in his pocket.

He scanned the back of the building. One door stood open.

"Lord, let it be the right one."

Dylan dashed to the door, but didn't go in. He stood to side of the open door to listen. He needed to know what was happening inside. One peek to see if Reggie had been shot.

He tucked his gun in the pocket of his jacket. He didn't want the gunman inside to know he had a weapon. The element of surprise was his friend.

He forced his breathing and his mind to slow down. Not the time to panic. Panic led to mistakes, and mistakes could cost Reggie her life.

****

"What's going on?" Robin yelled out from the

front of the gallery.

"Don't come back. Lock the door and call 911. Jeffrey's been shot." Reggie shouted.

The man cursed and rushed towards the showroom door and Robin.

Reggie ran to Jeffrey, moaning on the floor. Blood oozed from his shoulder.

Behind her, the man pounded on the door to the gallery's main room. *Thank you, God.*

Robin had locked it in time. At least she was safe.

She bent down, but Jeffrey pushed her away from him.

"Get out of here." Jeffrey whispered through his moans. "Go. Go."

"I can't leave you." Her voice broke and tears ran down her cheeks.

"Get out of here." Jeffrey moaned.

She looked at the gunman, still kicking the door to the gallery. She stood and backed towards the door.

The gunman turned. "If you take one more step, I'm going to shoot your friend again, and when I do, he won't be breathin' no more."

She couldn't let Jeffrey die. She stopped.

"That's a good girl. Now move away from the door." He motioned with his gun. "This won't take but a moment, and it'll all be over."

Reggie stared at Jeffrey. He motioned for her to run, but she shook her head. She wasn't leaving him to take her bullet. She took a deep breath and stepped away from the door and Jeffrey.

"Why are you doing this?" Her breath came in gasps as the tears continued.

"It's not personal. Just business, sweetheart." The man leered at her, making her feel dirty and cheap. "Course, we could make it personal if you want?"

Her heart thumped madly in her chest. Maybe she could save Jeffrey. She gave the man a look. "Let's go. Take me somewhere else. As long as you leave him alone I'll go with you without making a scene."

The man looked back and forth between her and Jeffrey.

She shuddered, but she had to get him away from Jeffrey.

The gunman stepped towards her.

Jeffrey moaned, but she ignored it. If she could get the man out of the room, her friend might live.

He grinned. In one swift movement, he grabbed her by the neck and turned her towards the back door. "OK, let's move it. I'll give you what you want. Your friend's life for a little fun. Sounds like a fair trade to me."

Her stomach heaved, and she felt a shudder deep in her soul. She refused to think of anything but getting him out of the gallery and away from Jeffrey. That was her only—

The back door opened. She turned her head an inch. Amazement and awe surged through her veins. No longer afraid, she took a deep breath. Reggie felt her captor's muscles tense.

Dylan's stepped into the room. His blue eyes met hers.

His hand rested in his coat pocket. Did he have a gun in there? Of course, he did. What was he even doing here? She'd told him it wouldn't work out, but he was here, anyway. He hadn't gone away.

"Why don't you just leave?" Dylan's voice was calm. "The cops will be here soon, and then it will be too late to leave. If you go now, you can still get away."

"Good idea." The man tightened his grip around Reggie's neck and pushed her forward.

Dylan shook his head, but stared deep into Reggie's eyes.

She would be OK. Dylan wouldn't let this man hurt her.

"You're not taking the lady with you."

Reggie's stomach churned. How could she have thought Dylan wasn't the right man for her? He would never leave her

"Yes, I am. She promised me a good time."

"Not going to happen. Just leave."

Dylan kept showing up every time she needed him. She wasn't worthy of him. Reggie stared at him. His hand was still in his pocket. Hope blossomed. Dylan could handle the situation.

She felt the gun move away from her head. Out of the corner of her eye, she could see the barrel pointed at Dylan. His hand moved from his pocket, a gun in his hand.

The two men stared at each other over gun barrels. The man's arm tightened around her neck.

"Looks like we've got ourselves a standoff." Dylan's attention remained focused on the man as he spoke.

"Yeah, but I've got the ace in the hole." The gunman pushed her forward a few more steps.

"Now, get away from the door and we'll leave."

Dylan took a step away from the door.

If she could only surprise the gunman in some way, then Dylan could handle the rest. She twisted ever so slightly towards him. He didn't notice. He pushed her forward another step, and as he did she turned closer into his body.

One more step. One more turn towards the man.

Reggie closed her eyes. She couldn't think about what might happen. Don't think about the gun pointed at Dylan. When she surprised the gunman, he might shoot Dylan. She couldn't bear the thought.

Maybe it would be better to do nothing, than risk Dylan getting shot. Just like Jeffrey. Her gaze found Jeffrey. He wasn't moving. *Oh, God, please let him be alive.*

"Dylan, just let us leave. Move away from the door." The words came out in a sob.

"You're not going anywhere." Dylan's gaze locked on hers urging her to go for it. The man pushed her forward another step. She turned closer into him.

Just do it. She took a deep breath, and in one quick movement, turned towards him the rest of the way and punched him in the stomach with all the strength she could muster.

He doubled over and his grip loosened. She twisted away from him, but lost her balance and fell to the floor. He cursed and swung the gun towards her.

30

He was going to shoot her. Kill her. In what seemed like slow motion, his finger pulled back on the trigger.

"Move, Reggie." Dylan yelled.

She scrambled to her knees and crawled.

Shots and more shots.

Reggie choked back her scream. Her gaze found the gunman. He lay crumpled on the floor. Dylan walked over and kicked the gun away from him. Then his arms were around her on the floor.

"Reggie, it's OK. You're safe." Dylan's voice penetrated the fog of fear. She felt safe—finally safe. This is where she belonged—in Dylan's arms. She wanted to stay there forever, never move again, but Jeffrey's moans brought her back to reality. She needed to help him.

"Jeffrey." Reggie whispered.

Dylan released her and she crawled over to her friend.

Before she reached him, the police burst in. A blur of blue. Screaming. Yelling. Guns pointed at her. Then at Dylan. Dylan tackled to the ground. She was yanked up and handcuffed. Paramedics rushed in. Jeffrey on a gurney. The gunman on a gurney.

Chaos reigned, but slowly order was restored.

Robin took control of the situation vouching for Reggie.

Reggie vouched for Dylan. They were both uncuffed.

Reggie sat on the edge of Jeffrey's chair staring at the pool of blood on the floor. No one else seemed to notice it. Jeffrey would be furious. Such a clean freak. The cup of coffee in her hand shook. Where had the coffee come from? Robin must have given it to her, but Reggie couldn't remember.

Had she thanked her? Reggie didn't think so. Tears flowed once again. She was sure she hadn't thanked Robin for the coffee.

Reggie searched the room.

Robin stood talking with an officer. Her hands moved through the air as she talked. She'd only celebrated her twentieth birthday a few months before. She must be terrified.

Reggie set down the coffee and walked over to Robin, wrapping the young college student in her arms. Tears. Whispers. More hugs.

****

Dylan watched Reggie comforting Jeffrey's young employee. She was the target of a killer, but there she stood comforting Robin, more interested in taking care of others than herself.

Reggie had told him she was selfish and self-centered, but he'd only seen the opposite since he'd met her. She had a heart. A big heart.

A policeman walked up and held out his hand to shake Dylan's. "Don't know if you remember me. Ray Davis from Alexis's condo the other day."

Officer Ray as Alexis and Reggie called him. Dylan nodded. "Sure. Is this part of your precinct?"

"Nah. My supervisor gave me permission to come here."

"Good to see you."

"We just got word. The gunman died on the operating table. We weren't able to get any information from him."

"Do you know who he was?"

"Gerard Hochs. He's wanted for several murders. His specialty is killing for hire. He mostly spends time between Cleveland, Pittsburgh, and Philadelphia."

Philadelphia. Where Stanley Federer lived. Dylan debated briefly whether to tell the officer about the Philadelphia connection, but decided to talk with Billy Clyde first.

"Just because he's dead doesn't mean Reggie is safe. We still don't know who he was working for."

"Yeah, I know. I didn't want to kill him but I had no choice."

Ray clasped him on the shoulder. "Don't worry. There shouldn't be any legal complications. It was a justified shooting."

"Good to hear."

"Reggie's going to need a safe place. The FBI's involved, now. They can find her a—"

"Not necessary, I'll handle it."

Reggie walked up to them and laid her hand on Dylan's arm. He smiled at her and put his arm around her waist pulling her close. She moved closer.

"Officer Davis was telling—"

"From the other day at Alexis's apartment."

"That's me." Davis nodded. "Reggie, I'm sorry you had to go through all this. I shouldn't have told you to come back until we had a confession. Dylan will tell you what's going on. You're both free to go."

"Really?" Reggie asked. "Dylan shouldn't get in any trouble. He was only protecting me."

"He's not in trouble. He may have to come for a hearing, but it will be a formality. Again, I'm sorry for what happened." Ray walked away.

"You OK?" Dylan's arm was still around Reggie's waist.

"We got an update on Jeffrey. He's going to be fine. Robin's amazing. She's refusing to close down the gallery while Jeffrey's in the hospital."

"You're amazing."

"Me." Reggie shook her head, running hands through her hair. "I'm a mess. You're the one who's amazing. If you hadn't been—"

"Not true, Reggie. You're the one that hauled off and slugged him. You should have seen the look on his face. You did good."

"You did good. You came charging in like a cowboy on a white horse. That was awfully brave of you." She nudged him in the side. "You must like me."

She had no idea.

"Just a little."

31

Reggie sat in Theresa and Billy's living room once again. Dylan stood behind her rubbing her shoulders. It felt heavenly. Why had she tried to chase Dylan away just the day before? Now, she couldn't imagine life without him.

When he'd shown up at Jeffrey's after she'd told him they didn't have a future, she knew she could count on him. That he would take care of her. Until she met him, she'd never had anyone she trusted completely.

"The only place you're safe is right here in this house with us." Billy paced the floor while the others watched him. "No one knows you're here or can connect you to us. And even if they could, they'd have a devil of a time finding this house."

Theresa nodded. "Or getting in once they did find it."

"That's for sure." Dylan said.

"I can't spend the rest of my life here." Realizing how ungrateful she sounded, she smiled. "Not that I don't enjoy your company."

"I guess we could give you a new identity and then you could go be free as a butterfly." Billy Clyde intertwined his massive thumbs and signed 'butterfly.'

Reggie looked at Theresa. "He's joking,

right?"

Theresa shrugged and glanced at her husband, then back at Reggie. "If you say so."

"I definitely don't want to know what you do for the government."

"I could tell you, but..."

Theresa walked over and punched her husband in the arm before he could finish the sentence.

"We're back at square one, I guess. I have no idea why someone feels it's so important to have me dead." Reggie reached behind her and grabbed Dylan's hand.

"It has to be about your father's money. Nothing else makes sense." Dylan moved from behind her chair and sat on the arm, letting his wrist rest on her shoulder.

Reggie opened her mouth to protest, but Dylan held up a hand. "I know you don't want to believe it but it really is the only thing that makes sense. There's no way Danny Jordan paid a professional hit man to kill you even if he had the money. His would have been a crime of passion. He would have done it himself."

"What should I do? Just call him up and ask why he wants me dead?"

"I think we need to be a bit more subtle than that. In fact, I have an idea." Billy Clyde cleared his throat dramatically. "Keep quiet and watch a master at work."

After punching numbers on his cell phone, he waited. "Yes, I'd like to speak to Stanley Federer. This is William Addams from It's Child Play."

When he hung up, Reggie shook a finger at

him.

"Billy, I'm surprised that you would lie."

"Who said I was lying? I told you I owned a small business."

"That's the company?" It's Child Play games and software were among the most popular games for preschool children, according to the computer expert who'd helped her pick out Christmas gifts she'd donated to children in the Giving Tree program last year.

"I needed a diversion from my serious work and my grandbabies needed some fun games that were educational. I never expected it to take off the way it has. We've been very blessed."

"Some diversion."

Dylan said, "I told you he was a—"

The phone rang. Billy handed it to Theresa. She answered using a professional secretary voice. She put the caller on hold, and then handed the phone to her husband.

After waiting a few moments, he clicked on the button. "Hello." He paused. "I wanted to talk with Mr. Federer, not one of his employees...I understand, but I'm interested in talking with him about selling my company. I could just put it on the market and let what happens happen, but I like your company and I'm going to be in Philadelphia this week. It would be a good time to explore my options with Mr. Federer." Billy gestured a thumbs up. "That would be wonderful. Let me give you my email address and you can send a confirmation along with directions."

After he snapped the cell phone shut, he stood up and took a bow. "Easy as pie."

Reggie stared at Billy Clyde then at Dylan. How had she managed to meet these amazing people? She knew they would say God arranged it. Maybe He had, but whatever it was, she was grateful.

"Now we need to make a plan." Dylan's expression turned serious. "And contact the FBI."

Billy Clyde walked over to the candy dish but before he could grab a handful, Theresa slid the dish from under his hand. He shook his head sadly and looked at Dylan. "We'll let them keep working their own angle, while we see if we get a hit on the hook we baited."

For the next hour, they brainstormed ideas about the face-to-face meeting with Reggie's biological father.

32

Reggie knocked on Dylan's hotel room door. After opening the door, he took one look at Reggie and burst out laughing.

"What's so funny?" She put her hand on her hips and looked over the top of the tortoise-shelled glasses.

"Nothing." He opened the door wider. "I wouldn't have recognized you if I'd walked past you on the street. It's amazing what glasses and a wig can do."

"Isn't it, though?" Theresa pushed past Reggie and walked in. "I may need to rethink my career options. I'm thinking I should become a makeover consultant. My motto can be from beautiful to nerd in a day."

Dylan laughed harder.

Reggie walked over to the mirror and gazed at her transformation once more. Theresa had done a great job. "You've got the talent, that's for sure. I couldn't have done it without you."

Before Dylan could close the door, Billy walked in. He stood staring at the new and, hopefully, unrecognizable Reggie, in her black wig sporting auburn highlights. Styled in a short bob, Theresa had combed it forward to better hide Reggie's face. She wore a shapeless dress that resembled a muumuu. Using makeup, Theresa had managed to make her so pale, she looked sickly.

"Whooeee. Great job, hon." He leaned down, picked up Theresa, and twirled her around as easily as if she were a child. "Let's take a look at some of my playthings, and then let's get this show on the road."

"I still don't know why I can't go inside with you." Theresa stuck out her lower lip in a pout. "I worked really hard to make Reggie look like that. I should get to see her in her acting debut."

"We've been over this. I need you in the van in case there's a problem, and I think four of us walking in would be intimidating and look suspicious. Reggie will be my ever-faithful secretary. Dylan's my assistant and—"

"I don't know why I can't be your attorney." Reggie interrupted. "After all, I am—"

"People, people, who is the director here?" Billy Clyde bellowed, and threw his hands up in the air as if he were the temperamental actor.

Theresa and Reggie fell into fits of giggles.

Billy rolled his eyes at Dylan who shrugged. Billy handed Reggie a notebook computer. "You will be taking notes on this baby, but it's no ordinary computer. It's networked to the computer in the van. Which means Theresa will be able to see and hear what's going on through the wide angle camera." He pointed to a spot on the computer's lid. The tiny webcam blended in so well that Reggie wouldn't have found it without him showing her.

She nodded.

"It has a microphone so Theresa will be able to hear everything going on in the room. The computer in the van will be recording the meeting as well."

"Isn't that illegal?" Reggie asked.

Billy Clyde gave her a look.

"Never mind. I withdraw the question."

"Theresa, if anything starts to bother you. And I mean anything. You call 911 on your cell phone."

"What should I tell them?"

"Whatever it takes to get the police there. I taped the address next to the computer in the van. Just in case you need it."

"I hate to be negative, but what happens if they take my computer?" Reggie's stomach lurched. She trusted Dylan and Billy but still…

"Why would they do that?" Billy asked. "Believe me. Stanley wants my company. There isn't any reason for him to think this is anything but a run-of-the-mill ordinary business meeting."

"It doesn't feel all that ordinary to me." Reggie sat on the bed. For the first time in her life, she would see her father. She wanted to look him in the eye and ask why he'd left her all those years ago. But that wouldn't happen today. Billy was clear that it was just a meeting to feel out the situation. This was Billy's show, and she'd follow the script he set up.

Billy showed Dylan and Reggie a small black device the size of a matchbook. In the center was a red button. He slipped one into the pocket of his suit coat and gave the other to Reggie. "If the situation turns dangerous hit the red button. Theresa's receiver will buzz and she'll know to call 911." He handed Theresa a larger black box. "This is the receiver."

"What about me? Don't you have any cool spy toys for me?" Dylan asked.

"These are not spy toys, Monroe. I just took some precautions in case there's a problem and yes, I do have a cool toy for you." He turned to the bed and pulled what looked like a squirt gun out of his briefcase. "Here's a nonmetal gun that can't be detected. Just in case we have to go through a metal detector."

Reggie eyed the gun. She hated guns, but after the past week, she had to admit they were necessary. She sighed. This might be one of those times.

Billy smiled at the group. "I don't expect any trouble."

"You don't expect trouble?" Reggie exclaimed, and rolled her eyes at Theresa. "I'd hate to see what you'd do if you did expect trouble."

"It's always good to be prepared. I think that's about it." Billy turned to Reggie. "It's not too late for you to back out. You can stay in the van with Theresa and still be able to see what's going on. Dylan and I can handle this on our own."

"I'm the one they're trying to kill. I want to be there."

"Reggie, you'll be safer in the van with Theresa. You can still see what's going on from the computer." Dylan sat on the bed beside her. "Billy Clyde and I can go in without you."

"Billy isn't expecting trouble." Her gaze bore a hole in Dylan. "Stop being such a worry wart."

"After what we've gone through the past

week, how can you even say that?"

Dylan was right. She should just stay in the van, but she refused to lose the chance to meet the man who fathered her and then abandoned her. She had to see what kind of monster he was.

"I'll be careful and you'll be right there with me." She looked Dylan squarely in the eyes. "But what you would do if you were in my position?"

"It doesn't matter what I—"

"That's what I thought. I'm going in with you."

"You tried, buddy. I could've told you she wouldn't listen." Billy turned to Dylan. "Reggie's tough."

"You say tough, I say stubborn, but it was worth a try." Dylan shook his head. "How's this going to play out? What are you going to say to the man?"

"We'll talk business for awhile, and then very delicately I'll ask him what's going to happen to my business if something should happen to him. Gotta make sure my baby's in good hands." He winked at Theresa. "My other baby."

"Good thing you added that, big boy."

"We're just there to feel out the situation and see if he's a good guy or a bad guy. Once we figure that out, we'll regroup and go from there." Billy looked at Reggie. "I mean it Reggie, this is not the time for a family feud. He is not to know that you're his daughter. I can't believe I'm letting you go in there." Billy held up a finger. "If you can't handle it, don't go."

Reggie stood tall and jutted out her chin. "I can do it."

33

Billy drove towards Stanley Federer's house while Reggie, Dylan, and Theresa sat in the back of the van. Reggie had never seen anything like it. Except in the movies. And that was how it felt, because things like this didn't happen to real people.

It seemed like an ordinary green utility van, but the inside had as much computer and surveillance equipment as what she imagined the FBI would have on a stakeout.

Maybe he really was a spy. Reggie kept the thought to herself.

Everyone appeared as nervous as she was. No one talked. She grasped Dylan's hand and every so often, he would squeeze it.

"We're approaching the house. Everyone knows what to do?" Billy called out from the driver's seat.

"We know, hon. You be careful in there. I love you," Theresa said.

After passing inspection at the locked gate, Billy Clyde drove up to the Federer mansion and parked as instructed. After Reggie and Dylan stepped out, Billy locked all the doors with Theresa safely inside.

Reggie walked behind the men as they led the

way to the door.

Before they could ring the doorbell, it opened. A tall, painfully thin, woman stared back at them. Auburn curls shot with flames of copper, hung below her shoulders.

Reggie felt even more frumpy next to the impeccably dressed woman, whose expensive dress hung limp on her bony frame. The woman stared, but didn't smile or speak to them. Her stone face was ghostly pale and pinched.

"I'm William Addams." Billy stepped forward. "I have an appointment with Mr. Federer." Billy offered his hand but all he received was another stare.

"Yes, I know." The woman sniffed as if smelling something foul. "I'm his daughter, Betsy Federer. He has health problems, but insisted on this meeting in spite of my objections. Please do not tire him out." Her upper lip attempted a smile, but it looked more like a snarl from a rabid dog.

"If it's a bad time, Betsy, we can—"

Talk about a lack of people skills. Reggie expected the woman to start foaming at the mouth.

Her model-thin frame shook along with her head. "It will always be a bad time. Don't you understand? He's sick. And he'll never get better." She glared at them as she stepped aside. "He wears out easily."

"We won't stay long." He motioned at Dylan and Reggie. "This is my assistant and my secretary."

Betsy scanned Dylan and Reggie saw the first hint of a smile. She finally shook hands with Billy Clyde and Dylan, but simply nodded at Reggie. If

Billy's information was right, Reggie was looking at her half-sister.

Did they look alike? Reggie looked at Betsy's eyes. Green, the same as hers. Her pulse raced. Her sister. The thought boggled her mind, but it was important to stay focused on the task at hand. She forced herself to remain objective.

"At least you agreed to meet Father here at the house." Her voice was void of any emotion and her eyes fluttered from Dylan to Billy.

Reggie dropped her gaze to the floor and swallowed hard. This was going to be more difficult than she realized.

Betsy motioned them into the house. A tasteful, but exquisite chandelier lit up the foyer, revealing a grand spiral staircase. Her mind flashed to the barren dorms she'd lived in as a child.

"Follow me." Betsy's heels clicked on tiled floor. They walked down the hall in silence. Betsy stopped, knocked, and then opened the door.

A man sat on the sofa but stood when the group entered the room. He was a small slender man. He looked as if he'd been ill for an extended time. Gray patches of hair mixed with shiny baldness. Unlike them, he was wearing jeans and a sweater with tennis shoes.

In spite of obvious signs of illness, his eyes were bright and friendly. He didn't look like a monster. He stepped forward with hand extended and smiled at them. "Good morning, Mr. Addams. I'm Stan. I've been following your company for some time. I've been looking forward to this meeting."

Billy shook hands. "Call me Bill. Good to meet you, Mr. Federer. This is my assistant, Dylan. He's just here to keep an eye on me. My secretary. She's going to be taking notes during the meeting if that's all right with you."

"Call me Stan. My father was Mr. Federer." He stepped forward and shook Dylan's hand, then moved towards Reggie with an outstretched hand.

She panicked at the thought of touching him. She moved back several steps. Realizing her mistake, she looked around and held the computer in front of her as if it were a shield. "Where would you like me to set this up, Mr. Federer?"

His eyes narrowed as he stared at her.

Her heart felt as if it might burst out of her chest. Good thing she had on such a shapeless dress. Otherwise, he'd see the rise and fall of her chest as she tried to gain control of her breathing.

Finally, he pointed to the conference table behind Reggie. "Right there's fine."

Rushing over to the table, she tripped, but caught herself before she or the computer landed on the floor. "I'm sorry. I'm just…"

"Are you all right?" Stan's voice was soft and gentle.

No, she wasn't all right. She should have stayed in the van. Dylan and Billy had warned her it might be difficult, but she thought she could handle it. She'd been wrong.

"I'm s…s…so s…s…sorry." Her face felt hot and her stomach queasy. There was nothing she could do now. She would have to get through this somehow.

"Nothing to apologize for." Her father's green eyes twinkled and then he turned back to Billy Clyde.

Dylan walked over to Reggie. As he helped her plug in the computer, he whispered, "Just take a few deep breaths. You're doing fine. Don't worry about it."

She nodded, but said nothing. Biting at her lip, she sat at the conference table and booted up as the men chatted. Turning on the webcam, she typed in a hello to Theresa, who responded back.

Reggie wanted to cheer. At least, the equipment worked, even if she couldn't stand on her own two feet. She looked up to find Stanley Federer staring at her. She forced a smile, then lowered her gaze back to the monitor.

When she looked back up, Stanley had turned his attention to Billy. "Would you like something to drink, Bill?"

"Sure, anything cold will be fine."

"What about you, Dylan?"

"No thank you, sir."

"And for you?" Stanley stared at Reggie. His words were soft and gentle, but his eyes probed her. She shook her head, not trusting her voice. She berated herself for being an emotional basket case. How was she ever going to be a litigator if she couldn't control her emotions better than this?

Stanley chose a seat facing Reggie. Billy and Dylan sat side by side on the sofa. A knock on the door drew the men's attention. Betsy walked in without waiting for an invitation.

"Can I help you, Betsy?" Her father asked.

"I thought you'd want me to sit in on the

meeting."

"It's not necessary, but thanks. You go have a good day. I'll see you later."

Betsy looked at the men and then at Reggie. She seemed hesitant to leave. She turned towards the door, but turned back to her father. "Are you sure? Maybe I should just—"

"I'm sure. We aren't making a deal today." Stan laughed. His eyes twinkled. "At least, I don't think so."

Betsy left with a last glance at Dylan. So, that was it, thought Reggie. Betsy found Dylan attractive. Not surprising. He was handsome, and even more so in the suit he was wearing.

Realizing she was staring at the closed door, Reggie turned back to the men. Again, Stanley's eyes were focused on her, but when she met his gaze, he turned back to Billy.

Billy talked about his reasons for considering selling his software company. He sounded convincing. Maybe he really was thinking about selling. Playing her role, she typed. Every now and then, Theresa would IM her.

Billy stopped talking. The room turned quiet. Finally, Reggie looked up. After several long moments, Stanley stood.

"I'm confused, Bill." Stanley Federer stood.

"About what?" Billy asked.

"About a great many things." He crossed the room to where Reggie sat.

Her pulse raced. Why was he walking towards her?

"What did you say your name was?"

Caught off guard, she looked at Billy, then at

Dylan, and then at Stanley. "You can call me Susan."

"How about I call you Regina? That is your name, isn't it? "The man's voice was cultured, but Reggie could hear the steel in it. "I don't know what game you people are playing, but I don't like it."

Silence filled the room. A sharp pain shot through her heart as Reggie heard her father say her name for the first time in her life. Dylan rushed to Reggie. He stood between her and Stanley Federer as if to shield her from any harm.

Billy stood and faced the man. "I can assure you this is no game, Mr. Federer."

"Why come here pretending to want to sell me your company? Why not just call and tell me that my daughter wants to meet me?"

"Because someone's trying to kill your daughter, and we thought it might be you," Billy said.

Stanley turned more pale than Reggie would have thought possible. He grabbed for the table. His breathing turned ragged and his knees buckled. Billy grabbed hold of the man before he collapsed to the floor.

He guided Stanley to the chair at the table.

Jumping up, Reggie rushed to grab a glass of water off the tray sitting on a side table. She reached towards him with shaking hands.

His hand shook as he reached towards her but instead of taking the glass. He touched her hand.

The glass slipped from her fingers and fell to the floor.

34

"Please forgive me. Please forgive me." Reggie's father dropped his head on the table, his breath ragged.

Was he admitting it? Had her own father hired someone to kill her? Reggie shuddered. He didn't look like a murderer. Dylan touched her shoulder. She stepped closer to him.

After a long pause, her father looked up at Reggie. He'd lost all color, tears stained his face. His eyes looked frantic and sad at the same time. He still held her hand.

Reggie felt his trembling. She tried not to feel sorry for the man. He didn't deserve her pity.

"I tried to do what was best for—"

"Best for you." Reggie pulled her hand back. How dare he act as if he ever cared about her or her well-being? "Certainly not best for me. I've spent my life thinking I wasn't good enough. That even my own mother didn't love me."

He winced with each word. "I just wanted to keep you safe. I thought I was doing the right thing." Stanley said. "I see now I made the wrong decisions, but I thought it was best…"

Safe? Best? She stared at him. She opened her mouth, but didn't know what to say. Nothing the man said made any sense.

Billy's cell phone buzzed, breaking the spell.

"We're fine. No need to call the police." Without another word, he closed his cell phone. "Let's calm all down a minute. Who were you trying to protect her from?"

"We need answers." Dylan caressed her shoulder and then pulled out a chair for her. He sat in another, scooted closer and kept her hand firmly in his.

Billy walked over and poured another glass of water and set it in front of Stan. Picking up the glass, Stanley's hand still shook. He took a drink then looked at Billy. "What do you mean, someone is trying to kill her?"

Reggie let out the breath she'd been holding.

"There have been several attempts on Reggie's life in the past week." Billy perched on the edge of the table. "The last one ended with the death of a professional hitman. Unfortunately, he died before we found out who hired him."

"It's my fault. My fault." Stanley's gray hair stuck out in every direction.

Her heart lurched.

"You wanted to kill me?" Reggie's voice shook.

Dylan squeezed her hand.

Stanley looked at Reggie with horror written across his face. "No, no. My dear, I only wanted to keep you safe."

"Why did you think she needed to be kept safe?" Dylan asked, impatience edging into his voice.

Ignoring Dylan, Stanley Federer continued to look at Reggie. "Did you really think that disguise would keep me from recognizing you?"

"We all did."

A hint of a smile crossed his face. "Your mother had auburn hair. With that wig, you looked just like Jeannie and just as beautiful."

She clutched Dylan's hand. He gave her a reassuring squeeze. This whole scene was so bizarre. It was as if the earth were spinning out of control. The only thing keeping her rooted in reality was Dylan's hand.

"I don't remember her at all. I had no idea what color my...my...her hair was. I've never even seen a picture of her."

Tears leaked from his worn face. He took a deep breath as if to compose himself. "I have a few. I will show them to you. I'm so sorry. After your mother's death, I thought the best thing would be for you to be as far away from me as possible."

"Dead?" Blood rushed to her head. She stood, but decided sitting was the better choice. Reggie stared at him. "I th...tho..thought she didn't want me. I thought she abandoned me."

Stanley stared at the ceiling, then looked back at Reggie. He shook his head. "No, no, no. You were the light of her life, but she needed to go see her father. I offered to hire a nurse for you but...she left you at the hospital instead. She was convinced it was the only place that could care for you properly because of your diabetes. She was killed before she could come back and get you."

Tears trickled down Reggie's cheeks, but she brushed them away. Her mother dead. And all these years she'd accused the woman of not caring. Just assumed she'd deserted her. Dylan handed her a napkin.

"I thought...I..." Reggie bit her lip. "I thought she didn't want me because of my diabetes."

"Absolutely not." The man shook his head. "She adored you."

Reggie's whole world shifted with his words. The beliefs she'd held her whole life were based on illusion, not reality. Her mother hadn't abandoned her. Her mother had loved her, had wanted her.

Sadness and anger melted away, replaced with grief. Her mother dead. Reggie struggled to keep her emotions in check. Too much to deal with. She would think about it later. For now, she had to find out who wanted her dead.

She wiped away the tears, took a deep breath and squeezed Dylan's hand. Reggie's eyes met her father's. "Why didn't you take care of me?"

Stanley stared at the floor for so long, she thought he wouldn't answer. His gaze moved up to meet hers. "I couldn't. I was married. It wouldn't have worked out. I thought it would be safer for you not be a part of my life."

"You keep saying that, but you aren't telling us why. You're not giving us the information we need." Dylan looked at the man.

Stanley's breathing was ragged. Reggie stared at him. He didn't look good.

"How did Reggie's mother die?" Dylan asked.

Gulping air, the man looked up. He looked as though he'd aged twenty years in the past ten minutes. "A hit and run accident."

A married man, with a mistress and an

illegitimate child. Life would be a lot less complicated with them out of the picture. She didn't want to ask but she had to. "Did you do it?"

He shook his head. "Of course not. I loved your mother. We were going to be married as soon as my divorce went through. But…but…after the accident…" He searched for the right words. "After the accident, I thought it better to stay with my wife."

Reggie's voice turned brittle. "Who killed my mother?"

His face contorted. He stood and walked to the window. The room was silent as they waited for his answer.

She couldn't take it anymore. She needed to do something while Stanley pulled himself together. She walked to the table, poured some water to sip, and forced herself to take a bite of the biscotti.

She heard a noise and turned. The door opened.

35

Betsy Federer walked in, but she wasn't alone. She held Theresa in a head lock with a gun pressed against her head.

Reggie's mind froze. Then, the panic broke through like water from a broken dam, threatening to drown her. How had Betsy even known Theresa sat in the van? A million thoughts bombarded Reggie's mind.

"My, my, what a touching scene. Father and daughter reunited at last. Daughter learns the truth that her mother and father loved her. That her father was willing to toss away his other children, his legitimate children, for his love child." The words spewed out like venom.

Dylan and Billy Clyde stood, remaining calm.

Not at all the way Reggie felt at the moment.

Neither man moved or reacted to the scene playing out. Reggie stared at the gun held against Theresa's head. Her mind flashed back to Jeffrey lying on the floor in a puddle of blood. She couldn't let someone else get hurt because of her.

She stepped towards her half-sister.

"Don't move," Betsy ordered. Her voice was colder than a prosecuting attorney asking for the death penalty. "Don't think I can't, or won't do it. All those fitness and self-defense classes Daddy's paid for over the years are finally going to pay off."

"Betsy, Betsy. What are you doing?" Her father stood, but held on to the table as if his legs wouldn't hold him up any longer. "Let that woman go before you hurt her. You don't have to do this. I love you." He implored her. "I've spent the last twenty-five years trying to prove it, but it's never been enough."

Betsy twisted Theresa's neck and Theresa yelped in pain. Out of the corner of her eye, Reggie saw Dylan step closer to Betsy.

Billy did the same on the opposite side of the table.

Betsy's face turned into a snarl. "It's not been enough because I knew you wanted her. You never wanted me. You were going to leave me."

Stanley looked like a broken man. His face showed the same anguish Reggie was feeling. "It's not true, Betsy. Just because I wanted to divorce your mother didn't mean I didn't love you and your brothers."

"Liar." She hissed through clenched teeth.

"The police?" Billy Clyde's mouthed to Theresa. Hope surged for a brief second until Theresa managed to shake her head.

Reggie's heart plummeted. They were on their own. No police were going to rush in and save the day. Her gaze met Theresa's. Theresa mouthed the words, "it's OK." But it wasn't OK. This was all her fault. She should never have agreed to come here.

She should have insisted they turn the information over to the police.

"No one can help you now, sister." Betsy's voice had turned shrill. "Good thing she called you on your cell phone, and I was able to figure out she was close by." She tapped the gun against Theresa's head with each word. "Otherwise, I might not have checked the van, and the police might be here at this very moment."

"It's not too late to stop this madness. No one is hurt. We can help you." Billy's voice drew Betsy's attention to him.

"How sweet of you to be concerned about me." Betsy's gaze fluttered between Billy and her father.

Dylan stepped closer to Betsy. Another and another. He was closer, but he needed to move faster—and without alarming Betsy

"Nobody wants to hurt you, Betsy." Billy's words poured out like warm syrup, soft and slow, and meant to calm.

Betsy laughed and pulled Theresa's head back further. Theresa grunted from the pain, but her eyes remained calm.

"Yeah, right. Do I look that stupid? But you're wrong. I am going to get away with this. Just like I always do." She laughed. "You people broke into our house to hurt my father. Pretending to own It's Child's Play. You were planning on kidnapping him for a ransom. I only did what I had to do to keep my Daddy safe. He'll back me up on this. He always does."

Stanley collapsed back in the chair and sobbed.

"But I do own the software company. It wasn't a lie." Billy Clyde stepped closer to Betsy. "The cops won't buy your story. They'll see it for what it is. Lies. The FBI knows we're here, today. You didn't think you could get away with all you did and they wouldn't find out."

Her eyes fluttered, and she looked confused. "Doesn't matter. Once the cops see your van, they'll know you were up to no good."

Dylan had managed to creep closer. Reggie needed to draw Betsy's attention away from Billy.

She stepped forward. "Betsy, it's me you want to hurt. Let her go."

Betsy glared at her.

Dylan and Billy Clyde both took another step forward. With each step, they closed the space around Betsy.

"Don't be ridiculous. If I let them go, they would tell the police." She shook her head. "And you're right. It's all your fault, you know. You shouldn't have brought them here. They're going to die because of you. "

Betsy looked at Billy. Her gaze flittered wildly. To her right, Dylan stood. She jerked the gun. "Don't you two even think about taking another step towards me. She won't survive a gunshot from this range. Back—"

Stanley stood, his voice strong in spite of the tears streaming down his face. "Stop this right now. It's finished, Betsy. I won't let you hurt anybody else. Put that gun down right this minute."

Betsy laughed. "You can't stop me. You've never been able to stop me. It's all your fault anyway. If you'd loved me none of this would have happened."

"Betsy. I—"

"Just shut up. I've had enough of you. I've spent my whole life trying to make you love me. But it was always about someone else. Mom, or Stan Junior, or her." Hatred spewed from her lips.

"You promis—"

"And I would have kept that promise except I happen to get a little peek at your will. I knew I couldn't trust you."

"My attorney has my will."

"Oh, please. It took all of five minutes to seduce that weakling. You were going to give her money—my money."

"It was just a small amount. You wouldn't have even noti—"

"That's not the point. You picked her again. You always picked her over me. It's always about her, her, her." Betsy screamed.

Reggie saw fresh hatred in Betsy's eyes. Without warning, Betsy pushed Theresa away and swung the gun towards Reggie. Billy grabbed his wife. Using his body as a shield, he rolled her away from Betsy.

Shots rang out.

Stanley Federer gasped and then moaned.

Betsy crumpled to the floor.

Reggie looked at Dylan, holding the gun Billy had given him. She took a breath and it was only then she felt the pain. She looked down as a circle of red formed on the front of her shirt.

Her gaze searched for Dylan.

36

Dylan sat in a private waiting room at the hospital, sandwiched between Billy and Theresa. It seemed like an eternity, but his watch showed it had been less than an hour since they arrived.

He looked down at his shirt. Blood. Reggie's blood. *God, please don't let her die.* He'd failed her, just like Daniella.

He shouldn't have let her go in. He'd been in tough situations before with Billy. Their connection was almost telepathic. He should have forbidden her to go in that house with them.

He shook his head and smiled. Reggie wouldn't let anybody forbid her to do anything at any time.

It would have only been another moment and they could have rushed her, but Reggie chose that same moment to draw Betsy's attention to her. She'd done it to save Theresa.

He opened his eyes and looked at Theresa. "Are you OK? I'm so sorry for getting you mixed up in this mess."

"You didn't get me mixed up. If you recall, I insisted on being part of the operation, darling."

Nice of her to let him off the hook, but it was his responsibility. "How'd she get you out of the van?"

"My own stupid fault. She knocked on the van door yelling her friend fell off her bike and needed help. Without thinking, I opened up the door and there she stood with a gun and that crazy smile."

"I should have given you a gun." Billy Clyde grumbled, as he enclosed his wife in his arms. "I'm never going to let you out of my sight again."

"I can't breathe, Billy." Theresa complained, but when he released her, she had a smile on her face.

"Please forgive me." Dylan looked at his two closest friends.

"Nothing to forgive, brother. You know that." Billy clasped Dylan's shoulder.

A doctor walked into the room and cleared his throat. He was tall and his blond hair stuck out from under the green surgical cap.

"I'm Dr. Langties. Mr. Federer said I'd find three very worried people out here, including the woman who saved his life. He's had a heart attack, but it looks as if he will be fine. His own cardiologist has arrived and taken over his case." He looked at Theresa. "If you hadn't been there, he wouldn't have survived. You did an excellent job."

Theresa nodded and wiped at her bloodshot eyes. "Thanks. Do you know anything about the woman with the gunshot wound?"

He shook his head. "I'm a heart specialist, but I'll go check."

Several minutes later, Dr. Langties reentered the room, his expression grim. "I'm sorry. She didn't make it. They did all that they could, but her injuries were too severe."

Theresa gasped and reached for Billy's hand.

Dylan voice was thick with emotion. "Reggie's gone." Theresa had warned him that even though the injuries didn't seem life threatening, gunshot wounds were always tricky, and even more so with diabetes.

"Reggie." The doctor shook his head. "Her name wasn't Reggie. Betsy Federer died from gunshot wounds."

"Not Reggie." Dylan mumbled and sat down on the chairs. Relief flooded through him, making him feel weak, but he still didn't know if Reggie would survive. He looked up at the doctor. "What about Reggie Meyers?"

"I didn't realize both gunshot wounds were connected with Mr. Federer. Let me check."

True to his word, Dr. Langties came back minutes later. "The doctors are still working on her. She's about to go up to surgery. You can see her for just a moment. If you're Dylan, she's been asking for you."

Dylan wasted no time. He jumped up and left the room before the doctor had finished talking. The doctor caught up with him and guided him to Reggie. They were wheeling her out of the room on a gurney, an IV attached to her arm.

Dr. Lanties touched his arm. "She'll be asleep in a moment. They've already started the anesthetic drip."

She smiled weakly at him and raised her hand. He grabbed hold. "I'm praying for you."

"Hurts." She mumbled through the drug induced haze.

He leaned down and kissed her cheek. "I love

you, Reggie."

"I love you, my cowboy."

Her eyes closed, but a smile graced her face. Her beautiful face. She'd said she loved him. She squeezed his fingers slightly, then her hand fell away as the drugs took full effect.

37

Four days later, Dylan paced the Philadelphia Medical Center lobby waiting for Reggie's release. The police had cleared him and the others of any charges. With the recording from Billy Clyde's computer, it was a clear case of a justifiable shooting.

Stanley Federer walked up. He didn't look like the same man Dylan met only days ago. Grief and regret had aged him to the point of almost being unrecognizable.

His hand trembled as he shook Dylan's. "It's all been arranged, the ambulance will take you to my private jet. Another ambulance will meet you at the Akron airport. I've arranged for a doctor to accompany you on the trip, in case of a relapse."

"Thanks. That's so kind of you. I also want to thank you for clearing me with the police."

"It's the least I could do. I should have hospitalized Betsy years ago, but I never had any real proof she was responsible for Jeannie's or her mother's deaths." His shoulders heaved. "I should have known."

"When it's all said and done, she was still your daughter. You didn't want to believe she could be capable of such acts." He left out the word evil.

"I tried to keep her on medication. How can I ask Reggie to forgive me when I can't forgive myself?"

"Reggie is a fighter, and the strongest woman I know." Dylan had a feeling she had more compassion than she realized. "Give her some time."

Stanley handed Dylan a large envelope. "When she feels up to reading it. It explains everything about Betsy's mental illness. I only wanted to keep Reggie away from Betsy. But I failed. I also included the pictures of her mother."

Dylan nodded.

Theresa and Billy walked up to them. "Where's our girl? Is she about ready to leave?" Billy asked.

"In a few minutes," Dylan answered.

"Then, it's time for me to leave. I don't want to agitate her." As Stanley Federer shook hands with each of them, he looked them in the eye and gave each of them an apology. He turned and walked away.

"That is one sad man," Theresa said when he was gone. "He is going to be in my prayers for a long time."

"It is sad." Billy Clyde said. "But that's what can happen when you use your money and power to keep your kids from facing the consequences of their actions."

"That's for sure." Dylan sighed. "If he'd gone to the police with his suspicions, life might have been different for all of them, especially for Reggie."

"Speaking of Reggie, there she is." Theresa

said.

Two attendants wheeled Reggie down the hall on a gurney. The gurney had been adjusted to allow her to sit up slightly. In her lap sat a huge bouquet of flowers.

Dylan leaned towards Billy Clyde. "I got her those flowers."

"Good job, Monroe. Women love things like that."

"Yes, they do," Theresa said and arched her brows at him. "Yes, they do."

"Don't you worry none, hon. Wait 'til you see what's waiting for you when I get you home." He leered at her. She laughed and punched him in the arm. "Billy Clyde, you are so bad."

Billy gave a theatrical sigh. "B-b-bad to the b-b-bone."

"Whatever." She turned to Reggie. "Hey, girlfriend. Howya doing?"

"I've been better, but I'll live, or so they say."

Dylan thought she looked beautiful in spite of her paleness.

Theresa grasped her hand. "Yes, you will. It's all those prayers that were sent up for you. You have no idea how many people around this country were praying for you."

Tears filled Reggie's eyes. "Thanks." She looked at Dylan. "Thanks for the flowers. They're beautiful."

"You're welcome, but their beauty doesn't compare to yours."

Reggie laughed. but winced in pain. "That's quite the line."

"I know. I read it in a book once and couldn't

wait 'til I could use it. I saved it just for you." The truth was, he'd saved his heart for her, but now wasn't the time to discuss it. He leaned down and brushed his lips against her cheek. Did she remember their declarations of love? He knew he'd meant his, but had she?

She touched her fingers to his cheek. "You are sweet."

He fought the urge to tell her once again of his love. It wasn't the right time.

She looked around.

"Your father just left." Dylan told her. "He didn't think you would want to see him."

"I wasn't looking for him." Reggie's eyes turned hard. "And he's right. I don't want to see him ever again."

Theresa patted her hand. "No one blames you for that."

"Everything's arranged for your flight home." Dylan smiled and brushed a strand of hair from her face. No need to tell her that Stanley had paid for it. "Are you ready to go?"

Reggie looked at Theresa and Billy. "Are you going with us?"

"No, we've got to get back home. Billy has things to do." Theresa told her. "I'd tell you what those things are, but…"

Reggie smiled, but it didn't reach her eyes. "Yeah, yeah, I know but then you'd have to kill me."

"Don't worry; we're going to make a trip up to Fredericksburg to see how you're doing real soon," Billy said.

"I can't believe…you've all done so much. I

can't find the words." Reggie looked at Theresa and Billy. "I don't deserve friends like you."

"Yes, you do." Dylan patted her shoulder. She deserved a wonderful life, and he wanted to be the one to give it to her, but that discussion would come later.

38

Dylan stood in his parent's dining room, now converted to Reggie's recovery room, and watched Reggie's closed eyelids. Her breathing was steady and peaceful and her color looked better than the last time he'd seen her. Careful not to disturb her, he closed the door and walked towards the kitchen.

His mom's voice drifted out to him as she sang. He smiled. He loved hearing her sing, but when she sang old hymns, it brought tears to his eyes. When he entered the kitchen, two cups of coffee sat on the table waiting.

She left the dirty dishes in the sink and walked to the table. The expression on her face said it all. She had something on her mind. No doubt about that. "How's Reggie doing?"

"Asleep now. She seems to be getting stronger every day."

His mother nodded and held up a pie pan. "Want some apple pie to go with the coffee?"

"Sounds great, Mom." He knew the small talk was leading up to the big talk, but that was fine. They could go at his mom's pace.

She walked over with a saucer filled with pie and set it down in front of him. She sat in her own chair and took a sip of coffee. "How are you doing?"

He lifted up the hot coffee and took a big gulp. "I'm fine. I'm not the one who got shot, remember?"

Mellie set the coffee mug down and stared at Dylan. "True, but if I recall correctly, falling in love can be almost as painful."

"It shows, does it?" Couldn't hide anything from her. She knew him too well.

She nodded but said nothing. She took a deep breath. Here goes, he thought. His mother wasn't one to mince words.

"I'm sure Reggie is a wonderful person but…" His mother's voice trailed off as she struggled to find the right words. "But I'm not sure she's the right woman for you, Dylan."

"I know things have been crazy the past few weeks, but—"

"It's not that Dylan. I'm glad you stepped up and helped her. In fact, I'm quite proud of my son, the hero. Daniella would be, too."

Their eyes met and he nodded. He'd known that wasn't the real problem. He stared at his mom waiting for the other shoe to drop. His mother wasn't known for being subtle when she thought her children were about to make stupid mistakes.

"Don't give me that innocent look, Dylan Charles Monroe. You know exactly what the problem is. She isn't a Christian. Now, I can, and do love, many people who aren't Christians, but it's never a good idea to marry—"

"I know." His voice was miserable. "It's not always easy to put God's wisdom into action."

Her words were gentle, but her point had

been made. "That doesn't mean it's hopeless. There's a little thing called time. Just ask your father."

"It's not like we need to get married tomorrow."

His mother laughed. "I hope not. You only met her a few weeks ago."

He took another bite, savoring the sweet cinnamon taste. "It seems as if I've known her forever."

His mother patted his hand. "It always does, dear. I know-"

Someone knocked on the kitchen door, and a moment later Joni walked in.

"Coffee's already made." Mellie said.

"No thanks. I'm too excited. Any coffee and I'll jump out of my skin."

Dylan laughed. "What's got you happier than an elephant with a bagful of peanuts?"

"Jeffrey sold all my paintings Reggie gave him."

"Oh, my goodness. That's wonderful." Mellie smiled. "I've always known God gave you such a gift with your artwork."

"I guess Jeffrey's feeling better. The last time I saw him he was on a gurney and on his way to the hospital." Dylan said.

"Much better." With a flourish, she pulled a check out of her shirt pocket and showed it to them. "Look at this."

Dylan whistled as he looked at the numbers. "No way. How'd he do that?"

Joni stuck her tongue out at him. "Maybe, I'm just that good. Did you think of that?"

"Oh, I know you're good, but that doesn't explain that much money."

"According to Jeffrey, he simply called several of his best customers and told them he'd discovered a fresh new talent. That's me. Once they saw my paintings they loved them. He gave them first option to buy with the understanding I would have a major art show within the next several months. He told them that he had no doubt that the value would more than double."

"Amazing. How's Richard feel about it?"

"He's thrilled. Really. He couldn't be more supportive."

My daughter, an artist." Mellie wiped tears away with the corner of her apron.

"Uh, oh. Mom's getting emotional." Dylan stood. "Time for me to go. That's wonderful, sis."

Joni wiped tears away. "You have no idea. This will get us back on track with our bills and we'll be able to give the kids a great Christmas. God is so amazing."

"Yes, He is." He leaned down and kissed his sister's cheek, glad things were turning around for her and Richard.

"This is an answered prayer." Joni closed her eyes and sat quietly for a few moments. When she opened her eyes, her smile was bright and light-hearted.

"Looks like Reggie could be the answer to more than one prayer." Dylan looked back towards the other end of the house. "I guess I better get going. I was hoping Reggie would wake up but I guess I'll have to wait."

"Good things come to those who wait." His

mother looked at him, her words thick with meaning.

He stared at his mother. She wasn't talking about waiting for Reggie to wake up. Reggie's injury gave him time to win her heart. *God, please soften her heart. I won't go against your word, but I sure do love her. She might not know it yet, but she sure does need me. And You.*

****

Reggie attempted to sit up but winced in pain. Never had she been so dependent on others and she hated it. *But how good of God to put these wonderful people in her life.* Wow. Where had that thought come from?

She shook her head. She'd never had a thought like that in her life. But with all that happened, she had to admit there was a God who loved her and answered prayers, after all. It had to be the reason she survived. There could be no other explanation.

"Knock. Knock."

Just hearing his voice made her smile. "Come in, Dylan."

He walked in with a huge bouquet of red roses, with tiny white baby's breath sprinkled in. Several vases already decorated her makeshift sick room. "These are for you."

"Dylan, it's not that I don't appreciate the beautiful flowers, but...," Reggie gestured around the room. "You've already given me more than enough."

"I know, but these are different."

She laughed. That's what he said every time he brought her another bouquet. "Why?"

"Because I'm here to declare my intentions to court you."

She giggled. Affecting a Scarlett O'Hara accent, she said, "Oh, you are. My, but that does sound like fun."

"More fun than you can imagine. And I have a surprise for you tonight, if you feeling like going out for awhile."

She clapped her hands. "Goody. I need some fun. It feels like I haven't been out of this room in a year."

"Good to hear. We're having dinner at my house. That is, if you're up to it." He set the flowers on the stand beside her hospital bed.

"I am so up for it, but I need clothes."

"Not to fear. Joni and I went to your apartment, and brought some clothes for you."

"I just can't believe all you and your family have done for me." He opened his mouth but before he could say anything she kept talking. "I know, I know. You say it's because you're Christians, but I've known other Christians and they didn't act like you and your family."

"Perhaps, we take loving others to the extreme, but it's what Jesus told us to do. We just follow his example as best we can. Believe me, we don't always succeed."

"I find that hard to believe. Your family has been unbelievably kind. You, I can understand, but your family. They are so special."

"They are special. God blessed me when He

stuck me with them. Of course, don't tell them I said that."

"I'm beginning to understand the love part, but what about all the rules you have to follow? Isn't that hard?"

He pulled the chair closer to her bed. "What kind of rules are those?"

She stammered. "I don't know but...but.. I know there are rules. You always hear about the rules."

He picked up her hand. "God has standards of behavior he expects us to follow, but...a lot of people have misconceptions about Christianity and rules. It's not the way you think."

Reggie yawned.

"Sorry to be keeping you awake. You need to rest. Time for me to go." Dylan announced.

"I'm sorry. It's not that I'm not interested. I'm just tired."

"See you later." He leaned over and kissed her lightly on the lips and left. She touched her lips and fell asleep smiling.

****

"I don't know why you keep that hair of yours straight. It's perfectly beautiful with its natural curl." Mellie said, as she sprayed conditioner into Reggie's hair and used her fingers to fluff it.

"People don't take me as seriously when my hair is curly." Reggie laughed as she heard her own words. "I know it sounds silly, but it's true. I'm a lawyer. I have to look and act serious."

"In that case, I'm glad I'm not a lawyer."

Mellie set the conditioner on the TV tray acting as a nightstand for Reggie.

Reggie was dressed for the evening events with time to spare.

Mellie held up a mirror.

"It looks great. Thanks, I couldn't have done it without you."

She hugged Reggie and sat down. "It's not a problem at all. I'm enjoying having you here."

"That's nice of you to say, but I'm planning on going home tomorrow."

"That's not a good idea."

"Why not? I'd think you'd want to get your family room back."

"I agree you're getting better, but I don't think it's a good idea to push your recovery. But the second and by far most important reason is that Christmas is in a few days."

"What's that got to do with me?"

Mellie clucked her tongue. "Because I want you to spend Christmas with us, of course. I think a much better plan is for us to go furniture shopping tomorrow. Dylan and some buddies can get rid of the old stuff. And by the time Christmas is over, your house will be livable again."

Overwhelmed by the love and acceptance of this family, Reggie sat quietly for several moments. Finally, she found her voice. "Mellie, can you tell me about Jesus?"

39

Reggie looked at her reflection in the mirror. Not bad for a sick woman. Her clothes hung loose. Getting shot wasn't the best way to lose weight, but apparently it worked.

"Are you decent?" Dylan called from the other side of the door.

"I am. Come in."

The door opened. Dylan wore a sweater and jeans. His hair had grown longer over the past few weeks and curlier. He looked good.

"Oh, darn. I was hoping I would get here early enough to—"

"You are so bad." She laughed as she stared up at him, delighted to see the love in his eyes. His lips found hers. After several sweet kisses, she stepped away.

He grinned. "I'm glad someone has some self-control."

She held up a hand. "Time for our first real date, mister. You promised me some wooing."

"And wooing you will get." He bowed formally at the waist. "Your chariot awaits you, my love."

After he helped her with her coat, he held out an arm and she put her own arm through his. They walked outside. The wind howled and the snow blew. Dylan looked at her and shrugged. "Welcome to Ohio."

She pulled her coat closer to her and snuggled into Dylan. "Where's your truck?"

"It's our first date. I thought it more appropriate to use my car."

"You have a car? I thought you only had the truck."

"It's quite the clunker and I love my truck, but it's not my only mode of transportation."

He pointed at a maroon sporty SUV. It was dotted with snowflakes but as far as she could see, it didn't have a bit of rust on the bumpers, nor a crack in the windshield.

"What? Did you think I was just some country hick who only had a pick-up?" He used a country drawl as he spoke.

She giggled. "Not at all."

He held the door open and she gratefully sat down, happy the car was warm and toasty. Just that short walk had tired her. He opened his own door and slid in. He gave her a quick kiss on her nose. "Buckle up."

"Oh, here we go again. It's the seatbelt cop in action."

"That's right and don't make me have to give you a ticket."

He drove down the bumpy drive and turned left. A few minutes later, he pulled into a drive. A beautiful two-story house with a wraparound porch stood in front of her. It was light blue with dark blue shutters adorning the windows.

She looked over at him. "You told me you lived in a trailer."

He smirked. "I said no such thing. I said a manufactured home."

Reggie bit her lip. "You know what I think? I think you deliberately tricked me."

"Did not."

"Did to. You wanted to see how I would react to you living in a trailer." And the truth was she'd been thinking like a snob, but loving Dylan had changed all that.

"You can't prove it, Ms. Lady Lawyer." He turned off the car and hopped out. In a second, he was at her side, opening her door. A blast of frigid air reminded her of the winter weather.

"I know what I know."

He grabbed her elbow and together they slogged their way up the sidewalk to his house. At the porch, she stopped walking, and started giggling.

What's so funny?" His warm breath tickled her neck.

"I guess I did have a few preconceived notions about farmers."

"You don't say." He laughed. "At least, you can admit it."

"Your home is beautiful, Dylan."

"Thanks. I'm hoping you'll like it."

His words made her pulse race as she wondered what he meant by them. He held the door and she walked into the foyer. He helped slip off her coat and led the way to the living room.

"Surprise." Voices called.

"Oh, my goodness." She gasped and looked around.

"Alexis, Jeffrey." Her friends came up and

hugged her. "Oh, Jeffrey. I'm so sorry about what happened to you. I can't believe—"

His brown eyes were cheerful as always. "It's not your fault, sweetie. I'm just glad we both survived. Such craziness. Can you believe it? I've been milking the media for lots of free publicity."

She laughed. Leave it to Jeffrey to find a way to capitalize on what happened. Alexis leaned in and whispered, "I brought Officer Ray with me."

"No way."

Alexis nodded, her eyes bright with happiness. "I think you'll like him."

Theresa and Billy were next. More tears. More hugs. Finally, they all sat down. Reggie looked at the group and began to cry. Dylan handed her a box of tissues.

"I'm sorry. I wish I could blame it on the drugs, but I've stopped taking the pain meds except at bed time. It's just me. I'm so blessed to have people like you in my life. The most amazing thing happened to me this afternoon."

40

Reggie sat on Dylan's porch, wrapped in a quilt, watching the snow falling. A white blanket covered the fields, making them glisten in the moonlight, reminding her of tiny diamonds. She held hands out, warming them on the blazing fire Dylan had made in an outdoor fire pit.

The day was perfect.

It was the kind of Christmas she'd fantasized about as a child, but never had. It had been filled with more love and laughter than she'd experienced in her lifetime. A tear trickled down her cheek, but she quickly wiped it away.

This wasn't a day for sadness. It was a day of joy. She was determined to live each day filled with peace and joy, knowing she was part of God's family.

Meeting Dylan had been the best thing that ever happened to her. God had been looking out for her when he'd let his truck slam into her Beemer. She smiled as she remembered how horrible she felt when she saw the crumpled red fender.

Dylan and his family had been so loving and kind. After learning the source of their love, she'd wanted it, too.

And now she had it. *Jesus.* She'd never

imagined she could feel so different, so loved, so peaceful, but she did.

Dylan walked out holding two steaming cups of hot chocolate filled to the brim. Three marshmallows floated on top of her cup, while his was piled high "Tired?"

"A little." She admitted. She sipped her hot chocolate, savoring the warmth and the sweetness. "But it's been a wonderful Christmas. I never had a Christmas like that before."

"The first of many for you, I predict." Dylan said. He sat his cup down on a small table between them. He added more wood to the fire. "Are you cold? We can go inside."

"No way, this is wonderful. It's so beautiful out here. It's a perfect ending to a perfect day."

He turned from the fire. "The day's not quite over." He picked up her hand and slid to his knees. "Reggie, I can't promise what the future holds, but I can promise I will love you with every breath I take for the rest of my life. Will you marry me?"

Her free hand flew up to her mouth. He pulled out a red velvet box and handed it to her. He flipped open the lid. A blue diamond solitaire surrounded by white diamonds glistened brighter than the falling snow.

Not sure if she could speak, she looked into Dylan's eyes.

"I picked a blue diamond because they aren't traditional and I wanted you to know you don't have to be a traditional farmer's wife. Will you marry me?"

Her heart leapt at his words. He understood

she couldn't be a farmer's wife. That she couldn't live down here in the middle of nowhere. Her heart soared. He understood and still he loved her. Life would be wonderful for them.

Tears of joy filled her eyes. *God, you have given me so much. You are so good to me.*

"Of course, I'll marry you. I love you."

Still on his knees, he moved towards her and their lips met. She hadn't known such joy and love existed. After the kiss, her cheeks were wet with happy tears. He slipped the ring out of the box and onto her finger.

Perfect fit. Holding it up to admire it, the yellows, reds, and oranges of the fire were reflected in it. The diamonds glittered even more because of her tears.

"I know it's really quick, but we can have a long engagement if you need more time. Personally, I'm in favor of short engagements so we can get to the honeymoon part, but that's just me." His hand caressed her hair and he pulled her to him.

When they parted, she nodded. "A short engagement sounds good to me."

He laughed. "Great minds think alike."

"What are your parents going to think?" Reggie's mind raced in a million different directions at once. So many questions filled her mind.

"They'll be worried we're rushing into things, but we know different. I promise to give you a life filled with wonderful surprises."

"And when we're old and gray, Can I remind you of that promise?"

"Absolutely."

Reggie admired her ring once again. "I know we've got things to work out, but I'm thinking you can go back to school while I work. We can live on my salary until you're finis—"

"Why would I go back to school? I'm a farmer." A look of confusion crossed his face.

A shard of fear pierced her heart, but she found courage to explain. "But I thought you said you understood I couldn't be a farmer's wife."

They looked at each other. Her stomach knotted as Dylan spoke, "I said I knew you couldn't be a traditional farmer's wife, but I'm a farmer. That makes you a farmer's wife by default. I don't expect you to do anything around the farm, and you certainly can have a career, but this is where we'll live."

She felt a crack in her heart. Looking around, she saw nothing but snow covered fields with only the moon for light. She couldn't live out here. As beautiful as it was, it wasn't her world. She looked into the fire. It was too hard to look at him when she spoke. "I can't live out here." The crack in her heart grew wider. "My job, my career's in Cleveland."

He stared out at the snowflakes falling. "But I have to live out here. This is where I farm. This is where my family is. This is where I belong."

She closed her eyes, her heart breaking. Maybe she could change. She opened her eyes and looked out at the empty fields. Maybe she could, but not that much.

She looked down at the blue diamond ring and touched it.

"Don't, Reggie. Don't take off the ring." Dylan's voice cracked. "Let's pray about this."

She wiped at the tears and nodded. She clutched his hand as if she was drowning and he was the life raft. How would she live without him? As he prayed she remembered Theresa's words, *I couldn't be happy anywhere without Billy, but I can be happy anywhere with him.*

Reggie felt peace flooding in her soul. Simple words, but there was truth in them, God's truth. *Is that your answer God?* A smile formed on her lips and in her heart. She had no idea how this was going to work, but she trusted God to work out the details.

She opened her eyes and moved closer to Dylan and touched his lips with hers. His eyes flew open, but before he could speak, she said, "I will so marry you. I can't guarantee what kind of a farmer's wife I'll make, but I can promise I will love you forever and ever."

"Just a little?" He winked at her.

"Just a lot." Smiling, she slid down onto his lap and put her arms around him.

EPILOGUE

The organ music floated back to where Reggie stood in the back room of the church. No pre-wedding jitters for her. She was right where she wanted to be and she believed with all her heart where God wanted her to be.

Reggie adjusted her veil and looked at her reflection in the mirror one more time.

God had been so good to her. He'd erased all her mistakes of the past and given her a future she'd never had the courage to hope for, let alone believe in. Who would have ever thought her life could change so much because of one silly fender bender?

"I'm ready." She looked over at the man who would walk her down the aisle. It hadn't been an easy journey for the two of them, and they hadn't reached the final destination. She was sure there would be more bumps along the way, but they were making progress.

Stanley Federer took her hand and placed it on his arm. "Reggie, have I thanked you for this honor of walking you down the aisle. I know I don't—"

She shook her head and hushed him. "The past is in the past."

Smiling at each other, father and daughter

walked out of the room arm in arm. The bridal march began and the crowd rose to their feet. She stood at the threshold.

Her eyes met Dylan's. What an amazing man he was. She'd spent her life pursuing money and power, but now she knew God had so much more planned for her.

Love was what made life worth living.

And she would spend the rest of her life pursuing love.

Thank you for purchasing this White Rose Publishing title. For other inspirational stories of romance, please visit our on-line bookstore at
www.whiterosepublishing.com.

For questions or more information, contact us at titleadmin@whiterosepublishing.com.

White Rose Publishing
Where Faith is the Cornerstone of Love™
www.WhiteRosePublishing.com

May God's glory shine through
this inspirational work of fiction.

AMDG

CPSIA information can be obtained at www.ICGtesting.com
Printed in the USA
LVOW06s1510300514

387959LV00001B/57/P